LUCY MEETS

ARTIFICIAL

INTELLIGENCE

LUCY MEETS ARTIFICIAL INTELLIGENCE

Anandajit Goswami
&

Debashis Chakraborty

MyBooks Publication

First Published in October 2017

by

Think | Create | Publish

My Books Publication
publish@my-books.in

ISBN: 978-93-86474-34-6

eBook & Cover Design
DigiConv Technologies

LUCY MEETS ARTIFICIAL INTELLIGENCE

Anandajit Goswami

&

Debashis Chakraborty

MyBooks Publication

First Published in October 2017

by

My Books Publication
publish@my-books.in

ISBN: 978-93-86474-34-6

eBook & Cover Design
DigiConv Technologies

Dedicated to our Families.

LUCY'S JOURNEY: THE SECOND STEP

When George Bernard Shaw commented that, "We are made wise not by the recollection of our past, but by the responsibility for our future", he was laying greater focus on the societal responsibility in general. However, if the focus shifts on environmental sustainability and the associated concerns, considerations on both the past experiences and the future responsibilities can make mankind wiser immensely. The underlying reason is that environmental disasters happening in a country are often repeated there as well as elsewhere, which underlines the need for looking back to look beyond.

How Lucy, the protagonist of this novel, fits in the responsibility-sustainability narrative? Both of us traversed on a similar path along our academic journeys, spending the graduation and post-graduation days in Calcutta University and Centre for International Trade and Development, Jawaharlal Nehru University respectively. The (externally structured) commonality in educational training and the (unplanned but welcome) similarity in the thought process eventually led us to develop an inclination towards environmental economics in general and sustainability issues in particular. The initial academic love towards the subject slowly turned itself into a permanent affection. Consequently, the urge to publish pure academic papers was turning into a desire to spread the sense of responsibility and wisdom in the society. The everyday experiences only strengthened our resolve to this objective. For instance, even launch of the Swachh Bharat Mission and the detailed media coverage on the Paris Climate Change negotiations and commitments did not deter many people from throwing empty plastic packets from their moving cars or plastic bottles in forest areas or lakes. Also, the renewed focus on the Ganga Action Plan contributed little to stop many from releasing various forms of pollutants in the river. Similarly, the practice of burning of dry leaves in parks in urban areas and crop residues in rural fields and illegal sand mining from riverbeds regrettably continue in several parts of the country.

The scenario indeed made us wonder, what can spread the sense of responsibility across the society, making everybody realize that protection of the environment for the future generations, who do not possess voting rights today, indeed matters? From this perspective, chronicling the adventures of Lucy, the acronym for **L**ove-**U**nderstanding-**C**reation-**Y**outhfulness, the intrinsic qualities to enhance responsibility, has been a natural choice.

While describing the journey of Lucy, a particular line of thought came to our mind. What if we try to re-cast the question of responsibility by reversing the narrative, i.e., attempt to predict the perils the future holds for us if we do not make an effort to learn and correct the present today? Academics keep on running simulations with complex modelling techniques and try to predict how grave the climate change consequences might turn out to be under different scenarios, unless corrective steps are undertaken. But such technical analysis often fails to stimulate right emotions among the wider audience. Thus through the eyes of Lucy, we tried to project the expected future and once the first line was penned down, the narrative simply just compelled us to move along.

Due to the common cultural traits, our perception towards Lucy's journey has been shaped by several literary contributions in the field of science fiction that we have read in the past. Our first exposure to this branch of literature came through the writings of Premendra Mitra, Hemendra Kumar Ray, Satyajit Ray, Khitindranarayan Bhattacharya, Narayan Sanyal, Sunil Gangopadhyay, Shirshendu Mukhopadhyay, Adreesh Bardhan,

Anish Deb, Siddhartha Ghosh, and many others in Bengali. The experience started getting all the more fascinating through our eventual exposure to the classic ideas of H.G. Wells and Jules Verne, and subsequently to the rich body of works by Isaac Asimov, Arthur C. Clarke, Ray Bradbury, Douglas Adams and many other authors. While attempting to understand our future through the eyes of Lucy, the works of these maestros indeed motivated us to think differently. And the sustainability challenges in a dystopian period has been an additional dimension that we attempted to bring in the framework. The rich contributions by Nicholas Georgescu Roegen, the works of several scholars in the field of Ecological Economics, Stephen Hawking's seminal work, "Universe in a Nutshell and Grand Design" and the ideas of film directors like Neill Blomkamp, Wally Pfister, Alex Garland also deserve mention.

Last but not the least, we are indebted to Lewis Carroll and Sukumar Ray for their masterpieces, *Alice's Adventures in Wonderland and HaJaBaRaLa* respectively, which enabled us to stretch our imagination regarding the depth of the rabbit hole.

Securing sustainability tomorrow is all about taking the right decision today. In the course of developing the narrative, we have attempted to make Lucy and the readers feel the repercussions of certain decisions (not necessarily restricted to the environmental scenario) undertaken by several historic persons in the past. The account of the events developed in the current context are purely fictional, and developed on the basis of our contemporary readings on those events. We particularly acknowledge our reading of the following volumes: *Return of a King: The Battle for Afghanistan*, by William Dalrymple, Bloomsbury Publishing, 2012 (for the incident involving General Pollock); *Prem* by Narayan Sanyal, New Age Publishers Pvt. Ltd., 2004 (for the incident involving General Choltitz); *The Impossible State: North Korea, Past and Future* by Victor Cha, Vintage Books, 2013 (for the incident involving North Korea); The *Anabasis of Alexander* (*The History of the Wars and Conquests of*

Alexander the Great) by Arrian of Nicomedia (translated by E. J. Chinnock), Project Gutenberg, 2014 (for the incident involving Alexander the Great) and *King Leopold's Ghost: A Story of Greed, Terror and Heroism in Colonial Africa* by Adam Hochschild, Pan Books, 1998 (for the incident involving Mr. Morel). And last but not the least, we acknowledge the deep influence of the Three Laws of Robotics developed by the maestro Asimov in his series of short stories and novels (for the basic principles guiding the AIs)

We also express our sincere gratitude to all the individuals who directly or indirectly have helped us during the course of writing this volume through passionate debates and engaging discussions in shaping our thought process on sustainability scenario. We are especially grateful to Mr. Prabir Sengupta for his constant encouragement in coming up with this book. The helpful and critical comments by the reviewers during various stages of this journey are gratefully acknowledged.

It is just not possible to adequately thank our respective family members for their constant support, bearing with our erratic writing schedule. Without that remarkable consistency in their support, this volume would never have come out.

As noted earlier, there is just one driving motive behind our initiative – to promote sustainable development. As the age-old adage suggests, 'Time and tide (which we may take as a metaphor of environmental disaster, and quite figuratively as the rise in sea level due to global warming) wait for none'. If the readers like Lucy's journey and take an effort in their personal life to practice the core sustainability principles before irreversible damage to the environment sets in, our efforts will be duly rewarded.

The helpful and critical comments by the reviewers during various stages of this journey are gratefully acknowledged.

Anandajit Goswami & Debashis Chakraborty

PROLOGUE

D r. Dang, a renowned scientist, always knew that the future for humanity will be a journey to leave the earth. His dreams of chilly wintry night of New York comprised of different juxtaposed images displaying strive of the human race, while settling in another planet.

His dreams also consisted of humans fighting for their survival in a changing climate. The dreams used to have *deja vu* of humans constantly struggling with another race who want a space on the Earth characterized by harsher climate and on the artificial satellite made by humans. He would get up early in the midnight with these images fresh in his mind, the nightmares often shattered by odd sounds from the neighbourhood. Whenever he would get up in the middle of the night, he would think - "Why am I getting these dreams? Who am I? Is there a purpose for which I am witnessing these strange dreams? Or, these dreams reveal images of a plausible future, accessed by a newfound psychic prowess that had been dormant so far?"

Often his thought process generated more questions than answers. With no satisfactory explanations, he would try to sleep and then often early in the morning he would proceed to his lab. Quite unknowingly, Dr. Dang had started believing in his sub-conscious mind that the future would unfold a struggle for space between humans and alien artificial intelligence (AI) entities in a dystopian background. The struggle between humans and AI would be all about to rule over the planet earth and understanding each other's' mind. This belief led Dr. Dang to explore, how and why all this would happen at the backdrop of changing climate on earth, with different dystopic elements.

Dr. Dang's ideas and convincing set of arguments found patient hearing in influential quarters and a huge research facility was set up to probe into these matters. While in public forums the research facility got prominence for its contributions in estimating adverse impacts of climate change, the secret experiments increasingly focused on simulations to learn from the future. Without knowing consciously, his experiments on Virtual Human Technologies quite silently had started to shift towards a world of dystopia with layers of struggle between human mind and AI. He gathered a team of like-minded people to collaborate with him in this endeavour. The experiments revealed that human mind is more powerful than sophisticated laboratory instruments in visualizing an alternate future. Through repeated simulations the protocols were standardized.

But why was this struggle necessary? This question used to bother Dr. Dang every day. He constantly questioned and always used to get lost in the trap of a rabbit hole of *Alice in Wonderland*. Then he would think and ask himself - "Are we all going to be like Alice in future when the survival of nature and human race will be at a stake? Is it that the imagination with an intent and resolve for course correction will be required then to give fruits to our new wisdom? What is required to come out of that rabbit hole where people like me got stuck mentally?"

To find an answer to these questions and fathom the immense possibilities that the future holds, Dr. Dang required a pure mind - a mind yet uncorrupted by the selfish interests, a mind that would view a scenario with amazement, curiosity, purity and try to find the virtues contained in it, rather than being judgemental. It was also realized through in-depth research that the pure mind of a child can project the images of a plausible future more accurately.

Lucy to Dr. Dang was a ladder to come out of that rabbit hole through the layers of sub-conscious mind. Through Lucy, Dr. Dang wanted to go deep into the mind layers and find out what challenges tomorrow holds for the human folk. He came to know that humans would try to adapt to the harsh climate change consequences, as an instrument to come out of the rabbit hole. He further sensed that, their own actions will shape their life long struggle for getting space on earth, and in other planets of the solar system when the nature and humanity's back will be on the wall. Hence, *Lucy and the Train* simulation was devised, with Lucy 'born' in the future in a train, which was moving on a track in an ice age akin to a dystopian wonderland. The track was actually a metaphor of time travel with loops and re-loops: as it is known that time can actually be imagined like a track with branches, loops and re-loops. So all these apprehensions of Dr. Dang culminated into the simulation of - *"Lucy and The Train"*. The future reflected in Lucy's mind provided the research team an insight on how to act today – it was a 'looking forward to look around and act' experience.

However, while Lucy was on the train, she moved forward and backward on time. She learnt how sustainability and various dimensions of it are joined together in the web of time and space. They often crossed path with each other, passed on the baton to one another in the continuation of time and space. Lucy learnt about it by meeting characters, through the questions and answers in the train. But she knew, this journey was the beginning and there were miles to go to know the next layer of plausible challenges humanity would create for themselves. So, Lucy's destiny through the time travel of the track and progressive experimentation was meant to meet various psychological layers of an AI, which was bound to shape life and choices of the mankind. Dr. Dang was more anxious to learn from the future mistakes, as reflected from Lucy's dream, and accordingly intervene to transform the alternate future in a more sustainable journey.

It was the AI, which was the rabbit hole of Dr. Dang and he wanted to come out of it for the future security of human race by means of Lucy. But sudden exposure of Lucy, a child of ten years, to complex scenarios may have been counterproductive. Hence a phased training schedule was devised. So - *"Lucy and The Train"* was required for "Lucy to meet the Artificial Intelligence" in order to understand the future of humanity in a dystopic world of future with various forms of social, political, psychological, economical and other varied uncertainties. Dr. Dang sincerely hoped that the opportunity to peek into the future would ensure a better today, and consequently, the tomorrow.

Hence, in the aftermath of the events described in '*Lucy and The Train*', Lucy was destined to meet the AI in the next layer of experiments. Dr. Dang hoped these experiments would enable one to peek into an even distant future. It is however observed that Dr. Dang grossly underestimated the ability of the alien AI mind to peek into the past.

THE TRAIN JOURNEY
CHANGES LUCY'S LIFE

D r. **Jonathan Dang,** better known as **Dr. Dang** to his colleagues, closes the lab and heads towards home. His daughter has been waiting since last few hours to enjoy dinner with her dad. Her dad was however busy completing the last legs of the experiment with Lucy in the train. Satisfied with the outcome of the experiment, Dr. Dang leaves the lab to head towards his car. He starts the car to rush for dinner with his daughter.

While driving he keeps thinking about Lucy's journey in the Train during the experiment. In the experiment the conscience of his daughter Lucy, after drinking ice cream and soda in the New York Central Park, was transported through a time-portal to a dystopian world in the plausible future. As the adverse effects of climate change cumulated, ice age had set in and mankind was forced to live in trains running in loops. There she went through a series of tests and finally, helped mankind to come out of the self-imposed unnatural confinement within a controlled environment. As per Lucy's choice, the mankind in the plausible future had to embrace the harsh and extreme climate to live in a sustainable manner. Dr. Dang keeps wondering how a second set of experiment can be conducted to understand the decisions that would be taken by mankind in the subsequent period, adjusting to live in the new environment. More importantly, he is eager to learn about the unsustainable practices that are going to be incurred in coming future, from the perspective of Lucy. This knowledge would prevent mankind from committing such mistakes tomorrow.

Dr. Dang's car is taking the last turn towards right that leads to the avenue in which his house is located. Suddenly, his car stops. The engine is not re-starting. Dr. Dang comes out of the car to check what was wrong with the engine. After coming out, he opens the bonnet and is trying to see whether any part is malfunctioning.

A hissing sound and a sparking laser pierces the silence prevailing at 11 p.m. in the avenues of New York. Dr. Dang is lying down on the road, in the pool of his own blood. He dies instantly as the laser ray that was aimed at his head, has successfully reached its target. As the echo of the sound faded, a deep silence returns to the streets and nobody is there to notice the crime. A stray beggar spots Dr. Dang's body after thirty minutes and alerts the police patrolling nearby in their night rounds.

The morning newspapers flashes the news of the mysterious death of Dr. Dang, the powerful and well-connected CEO of the Virtual Human Technologies with grave concern. The New Yorkers coming across the news story are only full of questions regarding the identity of the possible killer, wondering further for the underlying motive. A team of experienced NYPD (New York Police Department) detectives is appointed to investigate the matter. The unusual choice of weapon makes the investigating officers wonder about the identity of the murderer. A number of scientists, who ever had slightest tiffs with Dr. Dang are questioned.

***

It was 2015 when the crime took place. Since then one year have passed by but the killer is not yet found, even after intense investigation judging all possible motives.

In the meantime, the team that Dr. Dang had built up is now being led by his trusted Deputy, Dr. Jacob. Dr. Jacob is a very efficient scientist, and genuinely passionate on sustainability concerns, but he lacks the humane side of Dr. Dang in the management process of the simulation lab.

During one afternoon of September 2016, Dr. Jacob is taking a stock of the ongoing experiments in his office. He is engrossed in a number of folders full of papers spread on his table. With him is Dr. Chang, one of his colleagues, silently waiting for Dr. Jacob to finish his reading.

After a long time, Dr. Jacob looks up. After seeing Dr. Chang in front of him, he smiles faintly and says, 'Ah, I forgot that you are still here'.

Dr. Chang briefly nods, 'It's okay. I know the experiment results are mind-boggling'.

Dr. Jacob opens his spectacle and closes his eyes for a few seconds. The suddenly felt backache reminds him that he has not left his chair for the last four hours. 'It's not the right time yet.. I'll rest after a while', he silently promises himself with a sigh. Then with a renewed focus, he asks, 'So, let me know your perspective on the next course of action'.

Dr. Chang, who was preparing himself for this moment over the last few days, starts with a pained expression, 'I wish Dr. Dang were present today for this briefing'.

'Don't we all? Please continue.'

'Well, as per our earlier discussion, after the untimely demise of Dr. Dang last year, we have significantly improvised on the experiment protocol. The potions to secure transportation of the conscience are more powerful now, which enables the participants in the experiment to believe that they are actually a real person in the plausible future time frame. This we considered important, as an outsider would always carry his own perspective in the situation. In a sense he will still be guided by the thought process of the current century. On the other hand, a person thinking himself a natural resident of the experiment timeline would have no such inhibitions. Moreover, the laboratory equipment have been significantly upgraded, enabling us now to track the cerebral experience of the person's conscience to the minute details. Also we have closely monitored the mental growth of the children identified for the experiment. In the opinion of the team monitoring their behaviours and performances, they are ready for the second experiment.'

'Have you zeroed in on any particular test subject?'

Dr. Chang looks shocked and exclaims, 'Dr. Jacob! You are talking about ten year old kids..'

With a wave of hand, Dr. Jacob stops him, 'Spare me the civility part, Dr. Chang. We are all anxious to see the result. Dr. Dang's death was a big blow to the operations of this facility. Now the Board of Directors are demanding results. So, I repeat my question, any preference?'

'Well, the technical team confirmed that best results are guaranteed if only one child is allowed to participate in the experiment. And, if only one child has to participate, then I think Lucy happens to be the best option we have.'

'I too observed her closely over the past year. Initially she was too shocked with the death in the family. Now she has recovered to a large extent and in all probability is ready for the next experiment.'

Dr. Chang chews his upper lip in an uncertain manner for some time, as if he is trying to decide something. Dr. Jacob notices it and asks, 'What's bothering you'?

'You know, Lucy has not shared her experience during the first experiment with anybody. Her father died just after the experiment. The shock was too much for the child and she did not mention the incident to anybody since then. Not even her mother. Do you think it's right?'

Dr. Jacob gets up from his chair and walks to the window. He stares into the darkness outside for some time, before turning back to answer Dr. Chang.

'I've myself thought this over and over during the last few months'. He admits grudgingly. 'And my conclusion is we are actually better off, because the child had the prudence to maintain discretion'.

'What would have happened, if she had asked a friend to interpret the strange dream for her? They would just have laughed, shattering her confidence. Sharing with her mother perhaps? She has no idea about the minor details of our experiment. She might have taken her to a psychiatrist, who in all probability would have diagnosed this as an effect of the trauma she went through.'

'But she kept her silence and played the experiences in her mind a thousand times over the past one year. She must have come to certain conclusions on her own, without the unwanted influence of some grown-up's unnecessary intrusion in her thought process. What more do we want?' Dr. Jacob concluded in an air of finality in his voice.

After a few minutes silence, Dr. Jacob asks, 'How in your estimation the plausible future in Lucy's mind would be symmetric to the actual scenario?'

Dr. Chang smiles, 'There is no prior benchmark for us barring the first experiment. So, at best we can say fifty percent, perhaps. But nobody can give you a definitive number.'

Dr. Jacob grunts, 'I thought as much.'

Both the scientists read though the reports for a few minutes. Dr. Chang then looks up and sighs, 'So, what do you suggest'?

Dr. Jacob takes a deep breath and instructs, 'Start the process for second experiment from tomorrow. We'll proceed with Lucy only this time. Alert all our teams accordingly. I want to go for it within one month. Last time, we have developed certain ideas about the plausible future in 2150. This time, let us set the timeline a hundred years from that period, i.e., 2250. The target for us this time would be to see how the mankind adjusts itself to the changed environment. And of course to observe how Lucy, this time as a persona of the experiment timeline, interacts there and more importantly, intervenes.

Dr. Chang gets up for leaving and drily adds, 'Sure thing. Our team are also eagerly waiting to observe the next experience of Lucy'.

After his colleague leaves, under his breath, in an almost inaudible voice, Dr. Jacob mutters, 'And I will of course die to see if we can find the answers to a lot many questions.'

A SOCIAL VISIT

October 6, 2016

L ucy opens the front door of her residence and enters the hall. By habit, her eyes notices the digital wall clock. 4.30 p.m.

Earlier coming back from the school was like an opportunity, to drop the schoolbag at home and run to the Central Park. And add to that the lively discussions with her father during and after the dinner. If one day her father discussed the Hubble space telescope, the other day he would tell her unknown facts about the animal kingdom. She came to learn so many interesting facts about the likes of climate in Mars, Tasmanian devils, beavers, orangutans and so on. And some days she would listen to stories, with even the average ones transforming to special tales, aided by the witty and philosophical anecdotes from her father.

Now, sighs Lucy, the time is so different!

'My little princess is back!' Lucy's mother, a writer, comes out of the study and hugs her. She stares at Lucy for a few seconds and correctly senses her mood.

'Are you not going to play in the Park?'

'Nah! Not feeling like going there.'

'What do you plan to do then?'

'Maybe I'll read 'Alice in wonderland', that I've borrowed from the school library this week. The first few pages were so fascinating. I would love to see how deep the rabbit-hole goes.' Lucy answers.

Mrs. Jenny silently stares at her daughter Lucy for some time and then after a few moments of indecision, finally makes up her mind. 'Okay, you read the book for about an hour, after eating the meal I've kept for you on the dining table. After that we'll go to the house of one of the friends. They are asking us to drop in their place for quite some time.'

Lucy nods and complies with the instructions of her mother. At around 6.00 p.m., they leave their home and after twenty minutes of driving reach the house of Uncle Peter and Aunt Maria. Lucy remembers them, occasionally coming to their home for dinner. In fact, Uncle Peter happens to work in the same laboratory where her father was researching, and often spoke to him over phone during odd hours.

After initial chit-chat, Lucy's mother starts talking with Uncle Peter and Aunt Maria on many issues relating to sustainability, including forest fires, oil spills and so on. From her past experiences, Lucy is well aware of their passion on these subjects. After listening to them for some time, Lucy starts feeling a little bored.

Uncle Peter can sense her mood and asks, 'Want to watch the TV, dear? Or, you would like me to play a movie?'

Aunt Maria adds hurriedly, 'We only have books suitable for grown-ups, with lots of complex formulations. That'll not interest you either.'

Lucy weighs the options. What can be a good substitute for 'Alice in wonderland'? She suspects there is none.

Sensing the dilemma in her mind, Aunt Maria says, 'May I suggest a good movie for you? It has a young girl like you as a protagonist.'

'Okay, maybe I'll like that', Lucy thinks and nods.

Mrs. Jenny laughs and jokes, 'Knowing you, I presume there will be an environmental undercurrent as well.' Hearing this, both Uncle Peter and Aunt Maria also smiles.

Aunt Maria takes her to the room where there is a medium-size screen on the wall. She sets 'Battle for Terra' for play and leaves a big glass full of a fresh fruit juice on the table for her. Then she goes back to the room where Mrs. Jenny and Uncle Peter are passionately debating the possible extinction of bees and several other insects due to continuing deforestation drive and other man-made disasters.

Lucy is completely engrossed in the film from the very beginning. Once she finds the life of a human pilot in danger, she gets little tensed and starts drinking the fruit juice that was left on the table.

After a few moments, while watching the activities of the young alien girl, she suddenly feels that the surroundings are becoming blurred. Even the bright screen in front of her is not visible anymore. Slowly Lucy starts losing her consciousness.

LUCY'S DREAM: JOURNEY TO THE FUTURE

L ucy awakes with a start and feels something is echoing inside her head.

With the sudden uneasiness, she sits up to realize that she is lying on the floor. Surprised, she looks up and gets a shock. She is lying on the floor of a train!!

The train is not moving, but curiously, the sound of the wheels are still playing in the background. During half-sleep, the rhythm of that odd sound was reverberating in her head.

'I can't believe this..', Lucy exclaims suddenly, as she suddenly recognizes the place. It is the same train compartment where she opened her eyes last year, after eating the potion in the Central Park. Only this time the train is stationary and the lights are dimmer.

'Good, you recognize the place, then? Maybe you'll be able to remember me as well'.

Lucy is startled to hear a cheerful voice coming out of nowhere. Then with her eyes slowly adjusting with the dim lights in the compartment, she recognizes a human form standing up in one corner. The person slowly walks towards Lucy.

'You..' Lucy draws a sharp breath and stops mid-sentence, once the person stands next to her.

Lucy has every reason to feel puzzled. The person in front of her is none other than the balloon seller, whom Lucy first met in the Central Park last year and then in the train during 2150. Last time, reading from a diary kept in the train compartment, he narrated to Lucy the events that led to the environmental disaster.

Instinctively, Lucy starts looking around.

15

'What are you looking for, Lucy?' the balloon seller asks in a kind and knowing voice.

'The diary. You are going to read something to me once again, aren't you?'

The balloon seller laughs heartily.

'No, my dear. You see, history may repeat itself, but the future events may never occur in a similar fashion twice. Last time, the mankind was forced to live in a moving train. So, for the purpose of record-keeping and documentation, we stored the log of past events in the last compartment of the train. Today the humans do not live here anymore. That's why the train is standing. So, why should we keep the record here?'

Lucy nods. Yes, it makes sense.

With a twinkle in his eyes, the balloon seller asks, 'but you of course remember why we are not living in the train anymore, right?'

Lucy remembers her interactions with Lucas in the engine compartment during her last tryst with the plausible future society. Lucas was adamant that mankind should only remain within the safe walls of the train compartment. How she pleaded with him arguing, 'Humanity is the hope and not a train'. But all her arguments were falling to a pair of deaf years. So, she snatched the key and inserted the same into the keyhole, forcing the train to stop. It was implied that the humans would now try to settle on the ground.

'How differently would the future repeat itself this time? Rounds of quiz are awaiting me, I suppose.' Lucy mutters under her breath.

The balloon seller overhears her words and grins widely. 'No my dear, no quiz for you this time. More serious tasks await you.'

Lucy sighs. 'Looks like I do not have a choice. But before you proceed further, I want to ask you so many things. Since our last meeting, I am so worried about many things. First I want to know, why I am back here in this train. Second, my father..'

The balloon seller stops Lucy by raising his hand. His jovial mood is suddenly replaced by a weary expression.

'Lucy', he starts with a sense of urgency in his voice, 'I am truly sorry to cut you short. I wish I had the luxury to sit with you to explain all the thoughts and events that are bothering you. But I only have a short window to orient you for the next journey.

'Next journey!!' shouts Lucy in a bewildered voice. 'This is enough ..'

'Let me complete Lucy', the balloon seller urges, 'I'm here because you know me. All I can promise is that several queries you have in mind are going to be answered as you move along'.

Lucy is thoroughly unhappy, but she remains silent.

The balloon seller takes a deep breath. Then he brings out a piece of parchment from his pocket.

'This is 2250!! Can you believe this?' he announces in a mock cheerful tone.

Lucy is not impressed. She is still unhappy that the balloon seller is not ready to answer her questions now. 'Well, then?'

Sensing her displeasure, the balloon seller smiles sheepishly and starts narrating from the parchment.

After the ice age described in Lucy and the Train, the environment was changing rapidly from May 2150 onwards. The earth reached a phase where the heat of the Sun and meteor showers made it excessively warm. The heat thus generated melted the ice formed during the ice age and the wonderland was changing its texture. Additionally, the human-induced climate changes added to the worries. Now, the earth was increasingly becoming a mass of water with very less landmass. This was happening due to rising water levels from the melting of ice, which was flooding most of the landmass of earth. Besides, a series of earthquakes caused the tectonic plates to shift. Gradually, human habitat was located in one single landmass with the rest of the world submerged under water, barring the exception of very small islands, which were actually the peaks of large mountain ranges.

Several other changes were also happening in the plausible future, within the simulation experiment projection. In line with the change in texture, the world was witnessing many structural and sociological changes. It included settling of people of different income groups in the solitary landmass. The people belonging to the lowest income group were living as climate refugees there. Conversely, the people in elite or upper income group were able to create several smart island cities for themselves by reclaiming land from water. Such smart cities were characterized by patches of lush greenery, energy and resource efficient buildings, greater decentralization of power with most of the decision-making happening through online participation by stakeholders in these city councils and so on.

With a stark contrast, colonies of the climate refugees in the solitary land mass were dependent on politicians for every decision-making in their day to day life. Rent-seeking and corruption was rampant in these colonies to get any work done for the common mass, starting from getting a water connection to securing access to food.

With passage of time, a middle-income class emerged in the landmass who were living in places intermediate to the smart cities and the climate refugee colonies. No country emerged in this landmass as a political identity. Given the hardship prevalent in their living quarters, the middle income groups and climate refugees regularly dreamt of living in the smart cities, full of the amenities of life that they were deprived of. But they shared another grand dream as well!

They also dreamt to fly to a new artificial satellite outside earth, situated between their planet and moon. This satellite was built earlier by the humans from the elite income group.

So, human settlement was located in four regions, the smart islands named 'Eden', the satellite named 'Elios', the middle-income group's living quarters named 'Domus' and the climate refugee's settlement named 'The Reef'. The last two were located in the landmass.

The original goal of the elites was to eventually move out from the reclaimed islands, which was already a fragile climate. They also envisaged to build similar satellites further away from earth over a period, to facilitate this goal. The elites, who already separated their habitat from their lower income counterparts, was trying to secure a better lifestyle for themselves with a selfish standpoint. The satellite was characterized by the best of air quality, availability of water, health facilities for curing all diseases with gene therapy and organ transplants and so on, i.e., a modified environment promising humans a long, healthy and purposeful life.

But gradually this satellite came under control of the AI robots with human conscience, soul and sexuality. These AI robots came from another galaxy and gradually mixed with the human race settled in the satellite. After a difference of opinion arose on the galactic sustainability consequences with respect to the lifestyle and ethics of the satellite residents, the AI robots created a set of stringent rules. To get access to the superior facilities available on the satellite, human elites had to demonstrate to AIs that they rightfully deserve a place at the satellite due to their intellectual or scientific prowess and do not contribute to environmental degradation. Presently all the elite income group people even were driven out of satellite by AIs, as they did not stratify this basic requirement.

The artificial satellite is now being controlled by the AIs, with their leader Lazarus in command. Lazarus as a leader has the right mix of logical mind and rationality. The AIs on the satellite acknowledge that Lazarus has proved his leadership quality through his actions consistently over the period. Therefore Lazarus holds a strong control on his fellow AIs.

Forced to stay on the earth, the elites also wish to return to the satellite one day, a paradise in their narrative. Climate refugees belonging to the lowest income group on the other hand do not have that kind of money or opportunities to harness their true potentials, and their dream of reaching the satellite was practically unattainable. Similarly, the middle income group people are also increasingly aspiring to shift on the satellite, given the available amenities. All the groups are gradually becoming impatient.

With these developments, the landmass is becoming a fertile ground of conflict, as people belonging to each income groups are aiming to migrate to the satellite. To represent the voices of middle and refugee income groups, two spokespersons were identified and their abilities were accordingly harnessed. A need for negotiation to allow re-entry of humans to the satellite was perceived. With this common goal, the income groups started discussions among themselves. In these discussions, the middle income group is represented by Madhyam, while the climate refugees selected Bruke to be their representative. Both of them are admired by their respective compatriot groups for their selfless style of functioning and visionary qualities. The elites select Jack as their representative.

Jack is a renowned scientist, involved in research on generation of renewable energy. Though his inventions are appreciated by the elites, he is not considered to be a tough negotiator by the smart island residents. In particular, as he has never stayed on the satellite, the elites from Elios do not consider him sympathetic to their interest.

Madhyam happens to be a scholar, who initially worked in the university after completing his Ph.D and joined the council of the middle income group after some years. He lost his parents during his childhood and was raised by distant relatives. His abilities as well as selflessness and integrity were soon noticed and he was subsequently elected leader of the middle income council.

On the other hand, Bruke has very little formal education and changed jobs many times for earning his livelihood. He was separated from his family during an evacuation in his childhood, and presumably they died. At his middle-age, faced with the daily hardship and totally disillusioned with life around him, one day he suddenly realised the corrupt practices in all layers of the system can only be removed from within. So, he joined politics and after a prolonged struggle, came to power in his territory in the recent period. Faced with the daunting task of making regular public speeches, the realization that he is a gifted orator, was a surprise even to himself. However, he still prefers not to appear in many public functions, which creates an aura of secrecy around him.

In this contextual background of the world, protests emerged as daily features in the streets of middle-income and climate refugee colonies, demanding immediate initiation of a protocol permitting entry to more human folk from their quarters in the satellite. They were also blaming elites for the human-induced climate change impacts on satellite earlier and now on earth, leading to further discord among the human folk. Often violence was breaking out in these protests.

The balloon seller stops his narrative and looks up.

'Oh' Lucy exclaims, 'the stream of events are quite rich for me to digest. What can I, a ten year old girl, do in such a complex setting?'

In response, the balloon seller opens a box besides him and brings out a glass full of ice cream and a soda potion.

'Oh, not again', Lucy laments, realizing what is going to happen next.

'Patience, Lucy. You perfectly know that this potion would not harm you in any manner. It would on the other hand prepare your for the coming events to the desired extent.' The balloon seller soothingly notes, 'This will only change your persona to a young lady in her late 20s, who stays in a house near Madhyam. He happens to be a close friend of this new persona of you, Lucy. Now you'll be in a position to witness the negotiation and intervene if need be. This potion is just to ensure that you'll behave as a real persona of the current timeline.'

'So, I may need to snatch the key again?'

'Not figuratively, but metaphorically yes, such occasions may arise.' The balloon seller confirms rather happily.

Lucy just sits and stares in the near-dark compartment for some time. The dim light is creating strange patterns in the walls. Some are frightening.

Suddenly she makes up her mind and looks up. 'What's in it for me?'

The balloon seller answers in a reassuring voice, 'Although I cannot be too sure, my hunch is many of the doubts that you presently have, would be answered during this journey. In particular, the experiences would reveal to you the reason behind your return to this compartment and what happened to you father, in addition to the …'

Lucy does not want to hear any more. Snatching the glass from the hand of the balloon seller, she gulps the potion and a whirling tornado engulfs her. Slowly she loses consciousness once again.

DISCUSSIONS IN A PARK

January 31, 2250

Once awake, Lucy finds herself siting on a bench in a poorly maintained park. By looking up at the sun, she realizes that it is afternoon now. Barring a few small kids, nobody else is visible in the park. Someone is sitting besides her.

'What, you are not going to say hi to your friend, Madhyam?', the person sitting beside her asks in a deep baritone voice.

Startled, Lucy turns around to meet the smiling face of a stout young person in his mid-thirties.

'May I?' Madhyam asks and without waiting for the answer, sits closer.

After a few minutes of silence, Madhyam asks, 'So are you ready to join me in the negotiation of the Protocol with elites and the AIs that we are fighting for so many years?'

Lucy suddenly remembers. Yes, this is her friend Madhaym, back to secure a commitment from her that he asked last week. She counter-questions with some hesitation - 'But, why do you want me to join this protocol negotiation team'?

Madhyam dismisses the doubts in Lucy's voice with a wave of hand and answers in an amused tone - 'Lucy, who understands the mind of elites and the AIs' most? It's you, right!! - So Lucy, it has to be you! So without you how can we fight out this negotiation?'

'But how do you know that I understand the minds of the elites and AIs' most?' - Lucy again counters and waits for the response of Madhyam.

Madhyam gives a pause, thinks for a while and then responds with emphasis - 'Lucy you lost your parents early due in a climate disaster. Then you grew up in the community centre in my neighbourhood from your adolescence days to become an exceptionally sharp woman. Over the past 10 years I have seen your sheer brilliance with AI programming language through which you started creating mini AI robots since your college days. And today we all suspect that there might be an under the carpet tacit alliance between some of the elites and AIs of the satellite. So, we must have all the resources at our disposal to unearth such pacts, at every possible juncture.'

After a pause, he continues, 'So if we have to win this negotiation and create a world order of equality between elites, middle-income group people and climate refugees - we need you'. With more passion, he goes on, ' There is no second choice for us, if the AIs and elites prevail and enters into some convenient bilateral arrangement - that means disaster for us. Given the fragile climate we live in, we cannot afford to take that chance. Are you convinced now?'

'Ok' - a cold reply came from Lucy while Madhyam continues cajoling her hairs lightly with fingers.

Lucy remains lost in her thoughts for some time. After a while, she looks up and says, 'if I must prepare for the negotiation, I need to understand the nature of this ongoing conflict in the proper context. Though I know the bits and pieces of what transpired between humans and AIs in the past, can you recount them for me now?'

Madhyam smiles as he senses that Lucy's mind has already started preparing for the upcoming negotiation, which is good from his perspective. He gathers his thought for a while and then in a measured tone, starts his narrative.

'As the ice started melting from 2150 onwards, the landmass was visible once again. It was felt that as mankind had to endure a period of hardship in the trains, wiser with that experience, they will now invest every drop of their energy to lead a harmonious life. However, the sense of brotherhood did not last for long.'

'A group of people soon afterwards monopolized the available technology and emerged as elites. To escape the near barren landmass characterized by absence of scenic beauty, they resorted to an old form of technology called reclaiming of land from the seas, which was preserved in the train, for creating island cities. While the elites were happy with the green gardens and other amenities and luxuries created in those islands, it also led to loss of biodiversity in the sea. Additionally, several water sports and other forms of entertainment devised for recreation purposes in the elite smart cities led to re-emergence of not so sustainable practices once again'.

'Thus, the landmass became the home of all the lower income people, which means the ancestors of us. With passage of time, all the climate refugees from various parts of the world were rehabilitated here and they became the new low-income group. We, the original settlers in the landmass, now consider ourselves as the middle-income group.'

'The dynamics among the elites in the island soon led to formation of two groups there as well – elites and super-elites, and the latter group soon fancied a far more glamorous home for themselves. Their scientists intensified research to fulfil this dream. Subsequently, in the space, in a place between the earth and the moon, a new satellite was built in 2180, which relied on solar power. The satellite, constructed in the elite islands and then launched in the orbit, was found to support agriculture under controlled environment.'

'Initially the satellite was managed in a sustainable manner by the governing council elected therein. However, increasingly the super-elites from the reclaimed island was migrating there, to look at both the earth and moon through the windows of their not so humble abode. The growing population pressure led to construction of high-rise buildings and several amusement centres, not originally part of the master plan.'

Lucy unmindfully looks up towards the sky. She cannot help thinking how blue the sky looks. She wonders, how the earth may look like now from the space. Madhyam meanwhile goes on with his narrative.

'The life of the elites residing in the satellite was sailing smoothly until a fateful day in 2200, when a group of humanoid AIs from a planet of another galaxy arrived and questioned their urbanization drive. Initially the super-elites considered the arrival of AIs just as an opportunity for promoting inter-galactic commerce. However, an unnerving shock awaited them.

'Citing the present level of carbon and other harmful particle emissions caused by the increasing human settlement and amusement activities in the satellite, they explained the current growth rate of the satellite is going to cause an irreversible damage to the environment, affecting both the earth, the moon as well as the space. The AIs particularly questioned the environmental impact assessment system followed at the satellite while constructing the high-rise buildings and other economic centres. It was established through further probes conducted by the AIs that by paying bribe to the authorities, many super-elites have violated the existing norms, which has intensified pollution in the satellite on one hand and growing release of debris in the space on the other. Many super-elites deliberately did not undertake proper environmental compliance costs while constructing their homes, just to save money. This made economic sense to an individual with a narrow perspective, but was socially suboptimal with huge potential environmental implications.'

'After the initial shock, the super-elites tried their level best to convince the AIs that in coming future they will adopt every possible step to counter the environmental damage. However, the AIs rejected every argument. It was soon understood that they are guided by three basic principles. Number one, they try to protect every form of life, as that is crucial for the evolution and development process. Number two, they try to protect every habitable planet from irreversible environmental damage, because a new civilization can always evolve and grow there. Number three, if any conflict arises between principles one and two in a given scenario, they prefer to save the planet over people, because by their logic a civilization cannot exist without a habitat. So, if a set of life forms, whether intelligent or not, threaten the sustainability of a planet or the space, they prefer to relocate the species in another planet.'

'It emerged that the AIs and their creators were tracking the developments on earth for the last three millennium. The AIs, who were therefore perfectly aware of the earth's past track record in maintaining sustainability, were understandably not enthusiastic to believe that the super-elites in their own accord will adopt proper practices from now on. So, for management of the satellite, they formed a council consisting of representatives from both humans and AIs. The council after another round of investigations deported all the super-elites in March 2205 to earth, who flouted the environmental norms, or had some business links with the elites compromising on these fronts. Only the super-elites with proven track records of adopting sustainable practices and intellectual prowess like the scientists, were allowed to remain in the satellite.'

'The return of the super-elites to the smart island cities added the population pressure there and it also stirred the social structure the resident elites developed there since 2181. As a result, the demand for allowing them once again in the satellite intensified. Likewise, population growth in the middle and low-income colonies and the hardship there also fuelled the demand for resettlement of humans from these territories on the satellite'.

'But the AIs were not willing to allow more humans on the satellite. Things have particularly worsened since January 31, 2249 when all the remaining super-elites were forced to return from the satellite to the smart island cities. Even with their intellect and grasp of technology, they were no match with the AIs and felt that the council is not offering them a good deal. As the last batch of departing super-elites were not involved in the environmental damage scandal, they feel thoroughly betrayed by the AIs and are most vocal against them.'

'Furious, the super-elites toyed with the idea of creating another satellite in space. But the AIs objected to the idea stating that it can be equally polluting, and would thereby challenge galactic sustainability. They even explored the possibility to set up a colony in moon. But the AIs argued that the already fragile environment of earth's natural satellite cannot take consequent pollution load. Suddenly, despite the scientific progresses made, mankind has become a prisoner in their own planet.'

'So, the growing voice from all three colonies of earth is now loud enough for the AIs to not ignore. In particular, a number of elite scientists are now actively lobbying for allocation of more funds for building spaceships for going to Mars and Jupitar, where they want to set up human colonies. The AIs on the other hand feel that the human settlement in those planets might aggravate the pollution in space further and strongly oppose the initiative. So we are now going to initiate negotiations on a protocol for determining whether the humans, to begin with, can re-settle on the satellite once again.

'I suspect the residents of the island cities, elites or super-elites, do not really care for the others – but in order to show that the demand for allowing humans on the satellite are truly coming from all corners, they have not objected to the idea of having representatives from middle and low-income groups as well at the negotiating table. So, we have a council of earth now, with representatives from all three quarters. Jack and Bruke represent the elites and low-income group respectively. I, your friend, will be having the honour of representing the middle-income group.'

'So, I will soon go to the negotiation when the date, venue and place will be mutually agreed by the council of earth and AIs of satellites - and you are coming with me.'

After a few minutes, Madhyam turns back towards his home, leaving Lucy alone with her train of thoughts. The sun sets at the horizon and Lucy patiently waits to see the glimpse of moon in the sky. In the meantime, a ray of the dusky sun falls on her face. After an hour or so, she also gets up from the bench to go back home.

CALL OF THE ARTIFICIAL INTELLIGENCE FOR A NEW WORLD ORDER OF NEGOTIATION

Feb 1, 2250

azarus writes the last email of the day to Jack and leaves his office in the satellite headquarters. The emails are sent by virtual air driven digital platform. The senders just type on air and the texts are shown on the screen of the virtual air driven digital platform where the air itself is a mini computer monitor. Lazarus is pretty well versed with his skills on advanced technology as well as the ways of influencing people through his communications, including emails and personal interactions.

These discussions between Lazarus and Jack are going on for last one month since Jan 1, 2250. Lazarus feels that the humans who were driven out of the satellite one year back went to earth and started this movement against him by joining hands with Jack. These ousted humans were the super-elites who survived in the satellite as they were not caught in the corruption scandal of setting up high-rise buildings for themselves and causing damage to the environment by flouting norms.

After conducting a series of thorough environmental impact assessments from 2200 onwards, the council of satellite, through the influence and leadership of Lazarus, unanimously felt the humans caught in this scandal should be sent back to earth: a decision which was executed in 2205. The human beings who were not involved stayed in the satellite. These decisions were taken by the council of satellite which comprised of human beings and AIs. The council of satellite was further reporting to another council of AIs staying in another planet of a distant galaxy. The other galaxy council enjoyed a higher intellectual prowess through which they were controlling Lazarus, to whom all the AIs in the satellite reported.

As only the AIs were able to communicate to the higher council, they enjoyed the control of the satellite council. Gradually the power of AIs in the council of satellite increased. With the break-out of the environmental damage scandal in satellite, the moral position of the remaining super-elites was already weakened. The voice of humans in the decision making of the council of the satellite was gradually going down, in line with their economic prospects. The super-elites who stayed on in the satellite could not match with the AIs in terms of intellect. The AIs did nothing to reserve the trend. They started losing economic opportunities to the AIs and were finally forced to leave the satellite in January 2249. The AIs immediately facilitated the process, as though they were waiting for this to happen.

With all of these departed super-elites joining hands with Jack and trying to raise a new political movement against the AIs of satellite, during the last one month, the debates, discussions and arguments between Jack and Lazarus have increased. However, with respect to several decisions on environmental damage control, both on the earth and the satellite, they are not able to arrive at a consensus.

Lazarus feels that, Jack is also being provoked by the other income groups led by Madhyam and Bruke. Such provocation is leading to a constant demand by Jack for a new world order through a Protocol which will be negotiated between all the groups of earth, represented by a council of earth, and the satellite. Such a protocol will clearly decide the responsibilities as well as actions to be taken by each group to tackle the dystopic state of the world with a single land mass surrounded by water and a satellite with best of all facilities and nature.

Initially, the demand for this Protocol was put forward by Bruke. May be the income challenge and inequalities with respect to available amenities on earth between lower-income, middle-income and elites were contributing in driving this demand. However, Lazarus is not completely sure of that hypothesis even when he knows that a considerable time has to be spent from now on to find the basis for correcting the challenges related to the same.

But launch of the Protocol cannot be delayed any more. On earth, the income groups faced with the dystopic state had put the cultural identities at the backburner in terms of priorities for decision-making, despite economic and other existing differences. Particularly, the lowest income group led by Bruke was most vociferous about immediate launch of the Protocol, which has now gradually spread among the other groups too like a viral infection.

It has been a year since this demand was formally launched by Bruke. Meetings have been called by Jack many times where Bruke and Madhyam have also been invited. These meetings were officially called to discuss whether a Protocol is necessary to protect the single landmass and the satellite from human-induced impacts of climate change that have accumulated over the years and minutes of the meetings were duly forwarded to Lazarus. The meetings were held in the headquarters of the council of the earth which comprised of members from different income groups, in addition to the three nominated representatives. Unofficially the meetings devoted a great deal of time to strategize against the continued AI occupation of the satellite.

Aware of Jack's frequent meetings with Madhyam and Bruke, Lazarus tried to understand the needs of these income groups. Finally, Jack had put forward the demand for a Protocol to Lazarus for a peaceful coexistence of AIs and humans in the satellite once again given the dystopic state of earth. Following this, the debate between Jack and Lazarus became more frequent. After a month of discussion between Lazarus and Jack, Lazarus agreed to talk to the council of satellite regarding the launch of a negotiation for a Protocol.

Through a series of such meetings between the two councils, a consensus has finally emerged that there is a need to establish a Protocol between humans of earth and AIs of satellite to decide on the future responsibilities for addressing the impacts of climate change in a mutually acceptable manner and address the possible question of the return of the humans on the satellite.

While walking through the corridor, Lazarus sighs. There will be busy days ahead. His AI mind makes a note to speak to other leaders in the council of satellite next day.

LAZARUS'S DISCUSSION WITH COUNCIL OF SATELLITE

Feb 2, 2250

Next morning Lazarus summons the Deputy Council Chair of Satellite – Barbara to his office. Barbara was unanimously chosen as the Deputy Chair for her strong personality and rational decision-making capability.

After an hour long discussion, Barbara and Lazarus decides to officially announce the launch of a negotiation for a Protocol between humans of earth and the AIs of the satellite. Barbara and Lazarus select Raghav to represent AIs in the negotiation. Raghav, who was made in the satellite after 10 years of constant experimentation, is a humanoid AI with superior intelligence and knowledge about human conscious, unconscious and subconscious mind.

Once the formal discussion is over, Barbara gets up and asks, 'you are sure that conducting the negotiation on the basis of the results of a chess match will be a good idea'?

Lazarus nods and says, 'yes, I've studied the mind-set of the humans for quite some time. If we do not conduct the negotiation now, the discord between us will grow. If we just try to convince them through pure logic, they will always allege some plots and conspiracies, and disregard our arguments. Mankind has certain unique characteristics, often suffering from myopia.'

'Today Jack and other are negotiating with us in a sophisticated and formal manner. But if his approach does not bring the desired result, then a more militant group may seize control of the super-elites and may even try to launch an attack on us, despite their technological limitations. That'll simply pollute the planet further.'

'If we adopt any means during the negotiation that suits us, it'll never put a rest to this growing discord. Conduct negotiations with humans on the basis of facts, and they'll accuse arm-twisting! Present scientific data, they'll cry exaggeration of evidences!'

'Only if we can defeat them comprehensively through adoption of a convention that is aligned with their custom, we can hope to subdue their voices for relocation to the satellite, at least for some time.'

'Chess is THE tool, Barbara. It appeals to us naturally for the logical sequence, but it is not OUR game. Even the humans are aware that we do not play. It's not logical enough.'

'So, here we are appealing to their ego. Chess is being played in the planet earth for over a thousand years. They have a confidence that in their turf, an earth team WILL be invincible. And their lies our chance. They will not be able to refuse the result of an outright defeat in our hands in their game.'

Barbara persists, 'What if the humans refuse to link the results in a chess game and environmental sustainability together'?

Lazarus nods, 'I've weighed that possibility too. But from my understanding of the human psychology, it will not be a major concern. Mankind has no great proven track record of environmental sustainability during the last hundred years. Neither here on the satellite, nor on the planet earth. So, they'll actually be more uncomfortable to bring forward the sustainability issues on negotiations table. Trust me, this'll suit them better. Besides we are not deciding everything on the basis of the chess match's result. This is only a first movers' advantage that we are creating here. The side winning the match are submitting the first proposal. So the humans would believe that they can turn the table against us in the second round, where actual modalities of sustainability would be discussed, even if there is a setback in the chess game.'

Lazarus remains silent for a few minutes and then asks, 'hope my logical analysis of the human psychology is on right track'?

Barbara nods and says, 'as always'.

Lazarus then officially communicates the news of a launch of a negotiation for a Protocol to the representatives of various income groups on the earth through Jack. He also mentions that Raghav will represent the AIs in the negotiation and asks for nominations from the earth representing the elite, middle and lower income groups. Moreover, he adds a seemingly innocuous line, if the humans are defeated in the negotiation, some AIs reserve the right to settle on earth.

Barbara asks Lazarus after reading the line, 'So, we are now trying to save the planet earth from the polluting tendencies of mankind?'

Lazarus simply nods and clarifies, 'The overexploitation of resources today is setting in motion of the forces that led to formation of ice age in the earlier period. We cannot sit idle this time, given the fragile state of the environment.'

Jack asks for some time and conveys to Lazarus over electronic air communication that - "We will send you soon the nominations". He then discusses the matter with Madhyam and Bruke. The news breaks out on earth and all income groups start celebrating and begin their preparations for nomination. Once the initial euphoria subsides, a series of discussions start, as all of them are little unnerved with the potential implications of the AIs coming to live on planet earth, and what may follow subsequently.

After three days, the council on earth formally nominates Jack, Madhyam and Bruke for coordinating the negotiation. After a series of discussions with potential candidates, the three of them select N'Cono, who hails from super-elites, to be earth's representative.

Moreover, the council also decides to nominate a consulting team to accompany the three earth representatives in the negotiation. Through conversation with Madhyam, Lucy came to know that the team includes, among others, two persons named Eman and Ivan who are well versed with human scientific evolutionary history as well as various aspects of human brain. Eman hails from the smart island cities while Ivan comes from the locality of climate refugees.

The team members are selected on the basis of their abilities to complement each other's' capabilities. Lucy is included in the team for her expertise in computer applications and programming language. She has also recently started specializing in understanding AI codes. On the other hand, Eman is an expert of strategic thinking and started understanding the cognitive part of human brain. Ivan specializes in the non-cognitive learning abilities of human brain. Other team members have similar capabilities, which may be crucial during the negotiations. So all of them started specializing in the learning of different abilities that are expected to be useful in the negotiation process.

The council on earth subsequently starts their talk with the council of the satellite in order to mutually finalize a place where the negotiation will begin. The two councils decide on a gigantic ship as the venue of the negotiation. The ship is named as - "Noah" and can generate constant energy from water of the ocean and can stay afloat. The ship also comprises of an ecosystem of different temperature and climate zones that can sustain the survival of any species and habitation on earth.

THE TRAINING FOR
NEGOTIATION

March 2250

When Madhyam informed Lucy about her inclusion in the earth consulting team and its composition, she was not convinced about its strengths. Therefore, she suggested inclusion of another individual named Faith in the team. Faith, who was Lucy's classmate in the school, grew along with her in the ladder of education. Both Lucy and Faith learnt the techniques and AI programming language together.

There is a commonality between Lucy and Faith, which creates a strong bond between them. Lucy has no recollection of her parents. She was raised at the community centre of the colony of middle-income people. It was presumed that her parents died due to the climate change disaster, which was quite common at that time. Faith's parents were very much there for her, but after her twelfth birthday they never returned from a fishing trip at the sea. People wondered why they went for fishing after all, while there was a hurricane alert. After that Faith also came to live at the community centre and soon Lucy became her best friend.

In school all other students used to envy them for their acumen in understanding the AI programming. Gradually, both of them started experimenting with the assessment and understanding of the subconscious, conscious, unconscious mind of an AI. Each one of them created an AI prototype with an active conscious, subconscious and unconscious mind during their Masters, for which they were awarded high acclaims and were offered admission in the direct Ph.D. programme. Both Lucy and Faith completed their doctoral thesis also in understanding the application of conscious, subconscious and unconscious conscience in AIs.

Madhyam was also a scholar and received his Ph.D degree from the same University as of Lucy and Faith. All three of them were being noticed by the council of middle-income group for their academic, scholarly accomplishments and applied work in the field of application of AI. So when the negotiation was being planned, the council of the middle income group chose Madhyam, who according to them was the best, as their representative. In a short span of time, he was elected leader of the council. They also empowered Madhyam with the authority to select other representatives in the consulting team. As noted earlier Lucy was convinced by Madhyam to join his team and at her suggestion Faith joined later.

Madhyam, Lucy and Faith starts their preparation for the negotiation along with Eman and Ivan. To make the team conversant with the actions that are to follow for two weeks, Madhyam explains to the team the week-wise training schedule for the upcoming negotiation on the first day. Simultaneously, representatives from other income groups also will undergo similar training in their territories. To make optimum use of time, it was decided that the orientation programme for Eman and Ivan will focus more on developing their reading of the chess game. To complement their abilities, Lucy and Faith on the other hand will undergo a different training module.

'Week 1 will largely cover a training and discussion about the history and future of the satellite Protocol. Therefore, in week 1 we will discuss and learn about how the Protocol is an attempt to create a convergence between the income groups' - Madhyam briefs to Lucy and Faith. During the briefing by Madhyam, Lucy observes a sparkle in his eyes.

Faith remarks back to Madhyam - 'We should aim to create a chapter in the Protocol which ensures and recognizes a convergence between income groups and gives a binding to the income groups on securing sustainability on earth',

Lucy nods in assent. 'This will ensure that once we win the negotiation, there will be efficient distribution of responsibilities among various income groups', she adds.

Madhyam stays silent for some time, curling his lips, as if immersed in deep thought process. Finally he responds, - 'I totally agree…. But the AIs are making a demand that they can create such a chapter only when their ongoing experimentation on human moral boundaries and conscience are successful and they are able to create an optimal AI which is a prototype of human mind with the best of morality-based decision making abilities. Once such a prototype is cleared by the galactic council of the AI, only then they can create a chapter as suggested by both of you'.

'In effect, the AIs are bothered by the increasing environmental consequences of creation of newer smart islands by the elites. In their view, right now, mankind lacks the right awareness on sustainability. They believe just merely entering into a code on responsibilities of various income group will only result in a scenario like the last decade of Twentieth century, with no actual impact on the environment.'

'Tell me what do we do in this situation' - asks Madhyam, after being silent for a while.

'We should not give up our rightful demand' - Lucy suggests to Madhyam with her thumbs up. Nodding her ascent, Faith adds - 'If required, during our preparation after week 1, three of us can go through morality test simulation runs. I have heard about this simulations during our limited interactions with council of middle-income group. This would enhance our abilities to determine the correct course of action, whenever in a dilemma.'

'Precisely that is an integral part of our work plan is for Week 2, before we all join the negotiation in the ship. But I have to join the council of earth meetings. Both of you will undergo the simulation exercises.' - Madhyam replies with a smile and then continues to brief Lucy, Faith and others about the various aspects of the work plan in details.

WEEK 1: TRAINING ON HISTORY AND FUTURE OF THE SATELLITE PROTOCOL

Last Week of March 2250

The weekly training, as scheduled by the council of the middle-income group, starts from Monday, during the last week of March. The classes for the first week is held at the University from where Lucy, Madhyam and Faith obtained their Ph.D. degrees. Week 1 comprises of various discussion sessions covering the ongoing deliberations on the Protocol. It particularly covers the debates on the objective of the Protocol and possible future directions, particularly keeping the interests of the humans in mind.

Lucy has plenty of doubts in her mind. During the discussions, she asks the team of trainers a lot of questions on the reason why humans are trying to resolve the question of permitting entry to more human folk in the satellite through the Protocol. 'Is there no other option left to make the AIs agree to concede more ground to us?' she asks them repeatedly.

The lead trainer, a man named Rishi, smiles and says, 'Lucy, you must understand the scenario from their perspective as well, which is a crucial exercise in any negotiations. First and foremost, remember that the AIs have come a long distance, from a different galaxy, at a time when they felt that the human activities in the satellite are spreading adverse environmental consequences in the space. They have not come to take a 'no' from us as an answer. Second, they are technologically much superior to us in every aspect.

We cannot hope to force them either through coercion or by force. Besides, they are solely guided by reason and will not accept any argument that is not sustainable enough in their opinion.'

Lucy persists, 'But how does the Protocol fits in, in their scheme of things?'

Taking a deep breath, Rishi says, 'Look at the scenario from a Game theoretic standpoint. The Protocol is an equally probable event from the perspective of the AIs. They feel that while on one hand the Protocol may allow some humans to settle back in the satellite, their chance of getting a foothold on the earth is equally possible. If the humans go back to the satellite, they will surely not engage in activities like environmental scam again!! The lesson has already been learnt. And only a handful of super-elites may only go back to the satellite. Lazarus will surely control the entry in the satellite and will not let all the aspirants enter there.'

'On the other hand, the AIs may now try to wrestle permission to establish an AI colony on earth if they win. After settling in earth in case of their win, as per their practice, if they feel humans are polluting earth in an irreversible manner, they may ask us to leave our planet, just for the sake of saving it. So, while the Protocol is important, we, people of earth, participate in it only to win. A victory for the AIs will only mark the beginning of the end for us.'

Lucy remarks, 'What an extraordinary scenario'!

Rishi nods, 'Yes, it is.. If we reject the negotiation offer, then the rising population will only fuel discord among the humans. And the pressure on earth's resources further add to unsustainable practices. So, we cannot sit idle as that hurts us in the short run, and if we force a negotiation and be defeated, that'll surely hurt us in the long run!! But it is a chance that in my opinion we should take.'

Faith, who remained silent so far, asks with a little dull face, 'It seems from your answer that AIs are only a threat for us. Am I drawing the right conclusion?'

Rishi stares at them for a few seconds before answering, lost in deep thought. Finally he says, 'I will not say so. You see, one attempts to improvise only when there is a threat perception. Complacence leads to either mediocrity or disaster. If you look at the number of sustainability initiatives undertaken in the earth during the last couple of years, or since the beginning of our discussions with the AIs, the conclusion is obvious. So, while the arrival of the AIs have constrained our freedom of venturing out in space and increased the pollution abatement expenses in various walks of life, it has also made us aware of the limitations of our practices in no uncertain terms.'

'Perhaps since 2150, the humans were too busy battling the harsh atmosphere in the dystopian world, and too deeply engrossed in the struggle for securing basic amenities, often compromising on environmental front. Such practices indeed resulted in short term gains to earn livelihood. But at the same time in a way they were repeating the mistakes committed during Twentieth and Twenty-First centuries. The scholars decipher that trend clearly.'

'But what the humans strongly believe is that the sustainable path to be adopted should be determined by them alone, not by the AIs. A policy devised with satellite conditions or the one prevailing in the home planet of the AIs in mind as a model, will not improve the sustainability scenario here on earth. You need to understand this crucial difference in perspective.'

Lucy asks, 'If we win the chess game and put forward the demand for allowing humans once again at the satellite during negotiation, then only a handful of elites will get the chance to be there. What will be the benefits for the middle-income and low-income territories'?

Rishi thinks for a while before responding, 'I think technology flows from smart cities to the single landmass would deepen. The elites would want the migration of people from the smart cities to the satellites to be a regular affair. But the AIs comment on the overall sustainability concerns in planet earth, which lies well beyond their territories. So, they would want minimization of any form of environmental damage in the single landmass as well. The problem is, in the middle-income and low-income territories, production is labour and resource-intensive. Now, the elites would try their level best to improve that scenario.'

Faith comments, 'But they can always send outdated technologies'.

Rishi nods. 'Yes they can. But the fear of the AIs negotiating for a place in planet earth citing irreversible damage is far greater for them. Remember, we stay in the naturally formed landmass. The elites on the other hand have created the smart island cities. They cannot afford to lose them. So, in their own accord they are not expected to share a technology with us that maintains *status quo* here.'

After another hour's interaction, the session comes to an end. The discussions only strengthen Lucy's resolve on her quest to sustainability.

At the end of five days, Lucy, Faith, Eman and Ivan thank Rishi and prepare themselves for the next week.

WEEK 2: TRAINING ON "MORAL PSYCHOLOGY AND DIFFERENT MIND LAYERS"

First Week of April 2250

For the training of Week 2, Madhyam, Lucy and Faith are supposed to meet at the special training centre on the first day. The training centre was constructed by the council of earth almost two years back in a smart island city. It is only a 1 hour journey from the locality where Madhyam, Lucy and Faith reside.

Every day in the morning at 9 a.m., three of them are supposed to meet in the reception of the centre after crossing the security checks, showing their special card to the security guards. The council of earth provided the special cards to the members of the negotiation team. The other representatives, namely, Jack and Bruke and their team members also received similar cards and trained during different time slots according to their convenience.

This week, Lucy and Faith stay in the residential quarter of the campus as the trainings might stretch even upto late nights. The campus is a state of the art facility where energy from air, water, sun, moisture, grass, wastes from human and any other facilities within the campus is used.

On the first day, Madhyam reached the reception at sharp 9 a.m. The other two arrive late by 5 minutes.

Madhyam remarks in a grave tone after seeing them – 'This is unacceptable. Every day we have a plan of conducting at least 8 - 10 hours of simulation tests, followed by discussions. Each day we will have to go in one of the divisions of the centre and have to start different grades and degrees of morality simulation tests. How will we be covering that, if we are casual right from the beginning?'

Both Lucy and Faith sheepishly respond – 'We are sorry'.

'Ok, then let's begin' - exclaims Madhyam.

'You now have to undergo a specially devised set of simulation tests included in the training programme dealing with - "Moral psychology and different mind layers"', - completed Madhyam without a break, as if he has been waiting to convey this to Lucy and Faith for a long time.

'These simulation tests will take five days for both of you' - Madhyam announces as if like a doctor he was prescribing a course of treatment to Lucy and Faith.

Both women in an excited tone exclaims - ' We are looking forward to it'.

Lucy and Faith shortly afterwards arrive at the lab. They are introduced to the chief simulation scientist, Dr. Kate. After exchange of usual pleasantries, she then explains to Lucy and Faith - 'Here we will take you through real life visually animated virtual realities, where both of you will simultaneously be in different imaginary situations of the world with war, disasters, violence, love, unity, conflicts etc. In every such situation, both of you will be a protagonist and have to take decisions which are fair after the justice concerns are activated. Your decisions will be analysed to evaluate how the self-relevant value systems within both of you are working. It will also be seen how the various aspects of yourself viz. social, personal, moral and material are working behind a decision-making. Once the simulation is over, you need to explain the learning you had to the team. A score will come out after every simulation scenario is completed'.

'Each of the simulation situation will have a specialist with you, which happens to be Paul, who will discuss your experience with you so as to make your learning complete. This will also help both of you to understand how different aspects of your self-identity may lead to different degrees of fairness and unfairness in a decision making'.

'Wow, it sounds like we will go to a wonderland again' - Lucy says out of sheer joy of unexpected thrill and uncertainty. 'Even I feel so' - Faith backs Lucy.

So, both Lucy and Faith proceed to the simulation cubicle and a set of wires are attached to their heads. It is explained that they will participate in the simulations as one conscience, i.e., they will be present in a situation as if viewing the scenario through the two eyes of one individual. The person in charge of the operation, Paul, further explains that today the topic of the simulation will be *war*.

Once the rules of the simulation are explained in details, Lucy and Faith sit in their respective chairs and shortly afterwards their mind gets transported to the simulated scenario. The present completely fades from their minds. The scene emerging before their eyes first looks like a frame out of focus, images juxtaposed on each other. Slowly the view adjusts and suddenly the scene depicts high flames of fire engulfing several buildings. There are shouts of war, sound of gunfire, heart-wringing appeals for mercy and hoarse cries for help in agonized voices. Lucy and Faith look around in bewilderment. Where are they?

The misery and the abject destruction around makes Lucy and Faith to forget how the time is flying. They move aimlessly for several minutes. Suddenly a group of soldiers came running down the road. From the other direction, another group of officers came along. One of the officers from the first group salutes and reports, 'the order is being executed, Sir'.

The commanding officer, understood to be a General from his uniform, nods and tersely orders, 'let their lesson be complete.'

Lucy and Faith suddenly realize that they are entrapped in the mind of one of the surrounding officers. One of the officers from the group hesitantly and almost apologetically says, 'Sir, shall we really destroy the Chahr Chatta bazaar? The warriors fighting us have already fled. Why then shall we inflict further damage on the common people, affecting both a place of their livelihood and a historic symbol of the city?'

'Let it be done', roars the General, 'I want people of this land to get a clear message and never to forget the might of our power.'

Thus delivering his verdict, General Pollock moves on with his officers. A group of soldiers run towards the famous bazaar visible nearby for executing his order, with explosives.

By now Lucy and Faith have got a grasp of the ongoing event and wonder how to stop this. They look on helplessly for a moment and then their collective mind asks a fellow officer, 'But surely you cannot burn a bazaar, full with lots of inflammable substances? Imagine the degree of harmful emissions that you will be generating?'

The officer stares at Lucy-Faith for some time as if being asked the most stupid question. Then in an irritated voice he answers, 'Ahah, their country, their emission, their problem! And, harmful emissions, I say, what a fancy term indeed'. With this he sharply takes a turn and moves on.

Suddenly, Lucy and Faith realize that they are back in the simulation room. Looking at the clock they get really astonished, it seems like they have spent barely thirty minutes in the simulated scene, but actually it was more than five hours in the room. It feels strange, as if time was moving slowly for them.

The experience still haunting her, rising from the chair, Lucy shouts, 'how can they destroy a historic structure like the Chahr Chatta bazaar? Did they have no sense or compassion at all?'

Paul patiently answers, 'Lucy, the year you visited during the simulation was 1842. Colonialism was a dominant force. So, destruction and extraction of revenge after achieving victory in a battle was then often considered just a fact of life, however immoral and deplorable that may sound to us today. In the simulation experienced by your mind, Afghanistan just witnessed an action prompted by that mind-set. In your simulation, you only saw an approximate reproduction of the stream of events during that time.

Faith asks quietly, 'I presume environmental consequences were also of no concern in those days'?

Paul sadly adds, 'How do you think we arrived at the ice age situation in 2150? Remember, industrial revolution was still not there in full force in 1842. So, no country bothered to factor sustainability considerations in their actions, either undertaken in their home country or abroad. And of course, our world witness and suffer the results of their actions today.'

Lucy remains silent for a while and then asks, 'Is there a lesson for us to draw from today's simulation?'

Paul nods and smiles, 'Yes, there is. But why don't you figure it out yourself?'

Lucy looks towards Faith and with a silent twinkle in her eyes, she encourages her to answer.

Lucy then says without hesitation, 'today's lesson for me is to "PONDER". Before undertaking any decision, either in the time of peace or during conflict, all the possible repercussions, particularly the ones with sustainability implications, need to be weighed, appropriately considered and addressed. Otherwise, it leads to inevitable and irreversible destruction.'

Paul and other scientists gathered at the back of the room smile and their expression tells Lucy that her guess has been correct. Then the big screen in one side of the room glowed to life and shows a score of 9.4 out of 10! Lucy's reasoning and understanding is correct.

After few minutes of general discussions, they leave the room for taking rest and preparing for tomorrow. While there was least physical exertion, the simulation experience has been utterly exhausting for their mind, draining their energies completely. Still with the simulation memory fresh in their minds, Lucy and Faith have a silent dinner. In Lucy's dreams at night, atrocities committed in 1842 keep coming back repeatedly till she gets up in the early morning of Tuesday.

***

On, Tuesday Lucy and Faith eagerly reach the lab by 9 a.m. Paul informs them that the theme for today's simulation is *love*. They sit in the designated cubicle and the technical procedure is repeated.

Shortly afterwards Lucy and Faith find that the body through which they are viewing the scene is that of a military officer. The person walks amidst near-deserted roads where occasionally people are hurrying in a tensed manner. Occasional gunshots were heard in a distance. He finally enters through the gate of a building, named *Hotel Le Meurice* and goes straight to a room. He finds a soldier on duty there, who salutes and opens the door for him.

After entering the room, the person through whose eyes Lucy and Faith are viewing the scenario, sees that two persons are sitting in opposite ends of a big table. A General is sitting at the far end of the room. After the military salute, the person embodying the conscience of Lucy and Faith sits in the opposite end, besides another military officer.

Continuing the discussion, the other junior officer asks, 'But Sir, surely you are not going to disobey the direct orders of the Führer? How is that possible?'

General Dietrich von Choltitz gets up and walks around aimlessly in the room for a while. Then he comes back to his chair. It is evident that he is internally experiencing waves of conflicting emotions. In a low voice finally he says, 'Battle with the enemy, yes. Executing military strikes, yes. I will never dream of disobeying such orders. But leaving the city of Paris in complete rubble? Which means destroying Eiffel Tower, Louvre Museum, Notre Dame and other monuments? This is madness.'

The other officer persists, 'But this action will destroy the morale of the enemy.'

General Choltitz sharply reacts, 'on the contrary it will simply destroy whatever appreciation our administration and efficiency has ever gained. Besides, you cannot overlook geography. France and Germany will remain neighbours. This barbaric act will be remembered in history with profound ramifications.'

Lucy-Faith emphatically says at this juncture, 'General, I am completely in agreement with your judgement. We should not stoop to execute this kind of cultural atrocity.'

The other officer protests, 'But if the headquarter considers this act as insubordination?'

General Choltitz silently debates for a while and then making up his mind, solemnly says, 'Let history be a better judge of that. I will not be remembered as the destroyer of art and culture centres.'

At this point, the simulation gets over and Lucy and Faith are back in the lab. Though they are aware of the different pace of time in virtual and the real world, they cannot but feel amazed to see that more than four hours have passed since the beginning of the simulation.

The moments the wires are removed, Lucy asks Paul, 'I know the General did the right thing by not destroying the historical monuments and the crucial centres of art and culture. But how can we interpret the defiance otherwise? Particularly in light of the direct order he received from higher authorities.'

Paul thinks for a while and then answers, 'Lucy, in 1944, when the World War was in the last phase, nationalism was indeed a major sentiment running through the veins. But what we see is that General Choltitz did not look at the decision through the perspective of following the orders. He judged the scenario, not by simply considering the immediate outcome, but also what will be historical ramifications of his actions. If General Choltitz had destroyed Louvre, what would have happened to the masterpiece Mona Lisa? Unfortunately, in many other instances during that period, such restraint were not shown. So, why don't you draw for me the lesson from today's simulation?'

Lucy promptly answers, 'today's lesson for me is to "REASON". A person may be faced with a difficult circumstance, but only through logical and rational thinking he can deduce the correct course of action, that will not only be right in the current context, but also for the upcoming generations. This is the basic requirement for human progress and sustainability.'

Paul and other scientists nod in an approving manner and the session for the day ends. Before leaving, they do not forget to look towards the big screen, which displays a score of 9.6 out of 10 today.

***

Next day, the simulation starts at sharp 9 a.m. as usual and Paul informs that the subject for today is *conflict*.

The simulation takes Lucy and Faith to a rural area and they see that their embodiment, a middle-aged woman, is standing by the roadside. She is attired in modest clothes. A few persons seen around are walking and talking, but their actions are being undertaken in somewhat joyless manner. An air of gloom surrounds the area.

Lucy-Faith observes that the area has a few factories in the distance but no sound or steam was observed. With rising curiosity, they ask a passer-by in the voice of the lady, 'Why the factory is not operating? Is there a labour unrest?'

Hearing this the person literally shivers, shrugs his head vigorously and then almost runs away.

They meet a few other people on the way and find everybody quite scared to talk. Finally after a number of failed attempts, through the hurried and cryptic words of one person they realize that the reason is non-availability of electricity. Lucy and Faith are a little astonished but attributes it to some sudden disruption in power supply.

Proceeding further, they see an open field with a number of people gathering shrubs and a few people cutting the bushes. In places, they find evidence that a big tree has been felled recently.

The activities almost seem like an unplanned and unintended deforestation.

Lucy-Faith asks one person standing nearby, 'Why are the people cutting the trees?'

The man answered in a monosyllable, 'fuel'.

'What? Do you not have gas or solar power?'

'No', came the curt reply.

Lucy-Faith asks with more concern, 'For how long are the people cutting trees for fuel?'

'For some time', though the word count in the reply increased, it was still limited only to answering the question.

The curiosity level rising further, Lucy-Faith persists, 'Why there is no fuel?'

This time the villager looks on for some time so as to gauze whether the lady is seriously asking the questions or there are some ulterior motives. After much deliberations, he is able to assure himself of the true intentions of the lady standing in front of him and answers, 'Sanctions. No fuel.'

Lucy-Faith asks with rising interests, 'WHO has imposed sanctions on you? Why did they do so? Is it in response to any non-economic or unethical activities being undertaken in this country?'

This time with blazing eyes, the man shouted in a mode of lecture, 'No such activities. This is a conspiracy of the foreign countries against our beloved Supreme Leader. But the Democratic People's Republic of Korea will show to all our opponents that such measures cannot break our resolve. We will rise despite the odds.' And after completing the sentence, he hastily moves away from the scene.

Suddenly the barren fields make way for the simulation lab. Lucy and Faith realize that their exercises for today are over.

Once out of the simulation cubicle, Lucy utters, 'Paul, I do not understand. The country we saw, was unlike the other two experiences. It was not in war with another external enemy, at least tanks and gunfire were not around. Why then such sorry state of affairs persist?'

Smiling, as if he was expecting this question from Lucy, Paul responds, 'Lucy, in 1994, North Korea practically was not in war with any country, but it was technically not at peace with many of its neighbours, e.g., Republic of Korea, either. It earlier used to receive aid from countries like USSR, which in the post-1991 period was drastically reduced. Its own economic growth, because of the political and economic set-up and limited cooperation with the world was quite modest. Hence, capability for fuel import declined, electricity generation like hydropower projects reduced, as a result of which machinery sector was shrinking.'

Lucy asks with growing surprise, 'What did their government do to resolve it?'

Paul continues, 'The country was under sanctions for its conduct on supporting terrorism, outlook to nuclear tests etc. So, on the face of fuel deficiency, local people had no option but to cut trees, which in long run led to problems like land erosion and flood. If their Supreme Leader President Kim had been willing to amicably resolve the differences with neighbours through rounds of discussions, the problem could have been tackled. But their inflexibility on ideological grounds compounded the problem not only for the citizens but also for the environment. You see, focus on sustaining an ideology here clearly led to worsening of sustainability scenario. So, what in your opinion is the lesson from this simulation?'

Lucy thinks for a while and says, 'today's lesson for me is "OBJECTIVITY". A person or country needs to review a certain scenario not on the basis of their ideological standpoint, but from finding out a practical and sustainable outcome. Compromise on ideology with pure objective criteria in mind, like this case, is not a sign of weakness but indicative of the broad accommodative mind-set of the policymakers. Otherwise, it is a sure recipe for disaster.'

Paul shows a thumb-up sign with beaming face, signifying that Lucy's guess is correct. The display board of the big screen today reads a score of 9.7. The session for the day ends with everyone leaving the simulation lab.

***

On Thursday, at the simulation room, Paul tells Lucy and Faith that the subject for today is rejuvenation.

Lucy and Faith today finds them in a royal tent, implying that today they have reached a period way back in history. The tent is decorated well with valuable curtains and lots of cuisines are laid in front of the persons sitting in the room. A number of senior army officials are in the room and excitedly celebrating an occasion, probably a recent victory. Lucy-Faith see the event through the eyes of an army officer. In the middle of the room, sat a person who, despite his youthfulness, was obviously their ruler.

Suddenly he asks one of the generals surrounding him, 'Do you think our historians will place our victory today at battle of Hydaspes above Battle of Gaugamela?'

The general replies without any hesitation, 'O King, of course this victory will be considered a far greater achievement. Our army has depleted greatly since the battle with Darius. Many brave men have laid down their lives in the subsequent campaigns. Besides, we are fighting in a completely unknown territory now.'

Alexander the Great sat quietly for some time. Then in a distracted voice, he says, 'I cannot forget one thing. Darius fled from the battle, while Porus today stood until the end, even when many soldiers perished fighting by his side! I wonder, is it an act of bravery or sheer foolishness?'

All the generals merely nod, unsure what to say. Lucy-Faith suddenly exclaims, 'I will consider this as an act of honour, my King. Even after realizing the final outcome, he refused to desert his countrymen to their fate and stood by their side'.

Alexander chuckles and with a twinkle in his eyes, says, 'A Hector, you mean, eh?' After a few moments silence, he then commands, 'I want to see Porus right now. Bring him here.'

The wish of the emperor is executed, with Porus entering the tent with two guards shortly afterward. Sensing the mood of the emperor, one of the generals gestures the guards to leave them and wait outside the royal tent.

Alexander observes Porus intently for a few seconds, and then asks in a grave voice, 'Porus, you stand here today as a defeated ruler of a lost kingdom. How do you think we should be treating you?'

An interpreter duly translates the words. Porus, who so far has shown no sign of fear, answers in a matter of fact manner, 'obviously as an equal. Do not forget, o foreigner, I am *the* sovereign king of this land.'

After the words are hesitantly translated, there is a collective sound, as all the generals sharply draw their breath. What is the prisoner saying? Maybe he has never read *Iliad* and is blissfully unaware of *Hector's* fate. They all know that Alexander idolizes *Achilles* since his childhood.

Alexander, contrary to their expectation, suddenly bursts into a roar of laughter. Then he gets up and to everyone's surprise, moves forward to embrace Porus.

The surrounding lights suddenly became much brighter, too bright to be the glow of the burning torches. Lucy and Faith find themselves back in the simulation room.

Getting up, Lucy excitedly tells Paul, 'Such a majestic gesture by Alexander the Great! I am truly impressed by the conduct of both sides. Did all the kings usually extend such noble-hearted actions after their win in a battle?'

Paul smiles and replies, 'No Lucy, in around 326 BC and during later periods as well, in many cases the wining kings would kill their enemies and burn down their cities. Often, their decision was driven by the hatred for enemies, whose total destruction gave them the ultimate satisfaction. Sometime, the decision would be strategic, to refuse their enemies any opportunity of recover. You have yourself seen the response of General Pollock in Afghanistan at a much later date. Also, given the poor connectivity and transportation scenario and the limited knowledge-sharing due to language barriers in those days, cross-cultural interaction and understanding was quite moderate. We cannot really take pride in the practice of valuing human life in earlier days.'

Lucy thinks for a while and asks, 'So, Alexander the Great was different?'

This time Paul laughs heartily, as if he has heard a good joke. After a few seconds, he answers, 'Lucy, he did not earn the title 'Great' after his name for nothing. Imagine the campaign he commandeered at his age. Imagine the size of the landmass spread across Europe, Africa and Asia that acknowledged him as their emperor in his lifetime. Moreover, he was a wise person. At the time of the battle of Hydaspes, he was toying with the idea of going further east in India, with an aim to conquer the ancient kingdom of Magadha. Remember, he was far away from Macedonia, his kingdom, then. Having a friendly kingdom at his rear end was therefore a very pragmatic strategy. On the other hand, killing Porus would have only made his journey towards Magadha tougher, as all the kings on the way, aware of Porus's fate, would have fiercely fought with him. So, his decision was guided by a mature strategic mind set. But let me stop now, and listen to your analysis.'

Lucy remains silent for a minute before answering. Finally she says slowly, 'I was initially thinking that the lesson would be "COURAGE". Porus, a defeated king, demanded an equivalent treatment from the victor, an emperor with unparalleled authority ever in history. That was indeed a brave decision from his perspective. But then I realized that if Alexander the Great was not able to appreciate the true meaning of Porus's statement, such courage would have been wasted. It required empathy and understanding on behalf of both. Porus understood that only a true warrior will honour another and therefore did not hesitate to convey his expectation. On the other hand, Alexander understood that only a fearless soul, truly worthy of his friendship, not wrath, can make such a statement while being held a prisoner in enemy camp. So, for me the lesson for today in undoubtedly, 'UNDERSTANDING'.

The eyes of everybody present in the room reflexively turns towards the big screen. It reads 10 out of 10 today!!

Paul claps his hands in appreciation and utters, 'Well done Lucy. This is great!!! So, let's call it a day.'

***

And then comes the last day of the simulation, Friday. Lucy and Faith are quite thrilled, as today is the last day for the simulation exercises. They look forward to the final lesson. Paul, who now seems like a long-time friend to them, informs that today the simulation is on *violence*.

In the simulation, Lucy and Faith finds themselves in the mind of a dock official, moving in the wharf area of a port. The workers are moving the crates and boxes towards the ships. The area is having a strong smell of the sea and full of the regular dock activities. The man leisurely walks, occasionally wishing 'Good morning' in response to the salutations of some passer-by and finally enters a small office.

In the office, Lucy-Faith find two people talking there quite excitedly. The dock official, through whose mind they see the surroundings, is obviously known to both of them. He gently nods and joins the conversation.

One of the man says, 'Mr. Morel is making a very strong statement about the ethics of an operation in progress in Africa, in Congo to be precise, for some time. And just you hear the course of action he proposes in this regard.'

The dock official turns towards the gentleman named Morel

and airing the question of Lucy-Faith, asks jovially, 'What have you unearthed? Can I be privy to that information?'

Mr. Edmund Dene Morel gravely answers, 'Why, yes, indeed. In fact I intend to share the information with the entire world. I know it will be a shocker, but cannot really avoid that at any cost'.

The dock official asks, 'And what is that?'

Morel takes a deep breath and continues, 'During the course of my work and journalistic writings, I have come to know that the cargo carried by the ships traveling from Antwerp to Congo includes only arms and ammunition. It left me wondering who could be demanding these products in Congo, deep down the jungle. Initially I thought that it is entirely possible that some hunter was commissioning their delivery, but on second thoughts, the quantity was rather unusual. So I kept a cautious watch on the return cargo, which, to my surprise, included loads of raw rubber and ivory.

'Again, my initial thought was that perhaps barter trade is taking place and the price of the bullets and guns required for killing the elephants are being paid for in terms of the exports from Congo. But the repeat cargo movements made me suspicious. Clearly the cumulative value of the import of rubber and ivory, for so many consignments, far outweighs the value of the arms exported. Something does not match here. And when the information on the cargo somehow reached public forum, the sharp response of certain office bearers on my inquiry made me re-think on the possibilities. I have probed further on this matter. Considering every possible options, I concluded, the operations in Congo must be oppressing the local people, and in all probability forcing them to cultivate rubber, adding to their burden.'

Greatly intrigued, Lucy-Faith exclaims, 'Forced labour in Congo!! Shocking indeed. So, what do you plan to do?'

His facial expression hardening, Mr. Morel replies, 'I'll seek the answers from King Leopold's administration. If they try to evade the answers, I'll raise the matter in wider forum, and try to generate public opinion in other countries. Unless the matter is resolved, I'll not rest. No one can intimidate me in my pursuit for truth and justice.'

The scene before their eyes starts fading and Lucy and Faith are back in the simulation room.

With a heavy heart, Lucy sighs and says, 'Paul, why did such exploitative practices persist in the past?'

In a sad voice, Paul replies, 'Lucy, in late Nineteenth century, the growth engine of the colonial powers required precious raw materials. Obtaining them from the fertile lands of Africa and other continents with exploitation of the local people proved a profitable model for them in the short run, though by no means that can ever be considered as morally or ethically correct course of action. This particular operation in Congo was more of a private initiative rather than a concerted action by the colonial power. If profit motivations overshadow humane compassion, this is the outcome.'

Lucy persists, 'And the citizens of those countries did not object to such practices?'

Paul explains, 'You have to understand that the coverage of media in those days were not all encompassing, given the difficulties in sending news item on real time. Moreover, the exploitations were happening far away from the colonising country and many a times those news were not reaching the local populace. So, in short run people only noticed the economic growth around them, not the abject poverties persisting in faraway lands. But whenever it did, people like Mr. Morel did not hesitate to raise their concerns and seek justice. They were joined by like-minded people, cutting across borders. So, what do you think is the lesson from today's session?'

Without any hesitation, Lucy answers, 'today's lesson for me is "DUTY". Irrespective of the social or economic stature of a person committing a crime against humanity, it is the responsibility of a compassionate human being to stand up against that.'

Paul beams with pleasure and adds, 'brilliant, as always'.

Dutifully the big screen glows to life with a score of 9.7 out of 10.

Lucy thinks for a while and then asks Paul, 'I've understood the meaning of the individual lessons that we have learnt each day this week. Is there any broader understanding we are also expected to draw, based on our simulations during all five days, as well?'

Paul laughs and asks Faith, 'Lucy was conducting all the analysis so far. You like to conclude the overall lesson from these sessions?'

Faith smiles broadly and answers, 'Why, sure!! The overall lesson is P-R-O-U-D; the simulation exercise teaches us to **P**onder with **R**eason and **O**bjectivity whenever faced with a problem, so as to develop a complete **U**nderstanding and fulfil our **D**uty accordingly. Only that is going to make us – **PROUD** – and only then in turn the future generations will also be proud to honour our legacy.'

Everybody reflexively once again turn their head towards the big screen. It displays 10 out of 10 this time!!

After a while, shaking hands with Paul, Lucy and Faith leave the facility and on their way home discuss excitedly what the coming weeks have in store for them.

With the end of week 2, they receive a certificate from the special training centre confirming that they were now ready for participating in the negotiation platform.

Once back in their homes, Madhyam explains to Lucy and Faith that the primary responsibility of playing chess would rest with other members of the earth team. Lucy and Faith are expected to play a more important role, to analyse the behaviour, mindset and negotiating aspects of the AIs, once the next round of negotiations start. Their inclusion in the chess team is to enable them to observe the AIs on close quarters. Both the ladies agree with Madhyam's logic.

WAIT FOR THE CALL

April 2250

While, Faith and Lucy got the certificate, the Head Council of earth and satellite started preparing the venue for the negotiations. The news of the preparations came to Lucy and Faith everyday through their special virtual spectacles which were mini tablets in which information and virtual exchange can happen simultaneously. The wait became longer and longer for Lucy and Faith as weeks passed by. They knew they will be called anytime in the venue and all their expenses for travel, boarding and lodging will be borne by the council of Earth.

Meanwhile the fear that if the AIs win, they might displace earthmen from their territories, lead to a temporary truce between the elites and residents of the landmass. All the humans start supporting the negotiating team from their planet. The mutual mistrust did not totally disappear, but was temporarily shelved.

During this time before getting a call from the council, Lucy and Faith spend the first week studying the famous moves of chess maestros, including the likes of Bobby Fischer, Garry Kasparov, José Raúl Capablanca, Paul Morphy, Alexander Alekhine, Wilhelm Steinitz and many others. They were helped by Eman and Ivan, who had earlier spent the first week of April learning the chess moves. Sometime Madhyam joined them to encourage their preparation for the negotiation. Often they start playing after breakfast, the game dragging for the next five-six hours. While Faith is winning most of the time in the beginning, Lucy starts to win all the games towards the end of the week. On the other hand, Eman prevailed over Ivan in most of the games.

After two weeks of intensive practice, they start to feel the fatigue. Hence before getting a call from the council of earth, Lucy and Faith decides to chill out for a small vacation prior to going for the negotiation venue. They keep discussing the much-awaited break, but are indecisive about the appropriate venue of their vacation.

Every afternoon Lucy and Faith generally meet in the park of their locality as they both reside in the same neighbourhood. In one such afternoon, Lucy asks Faith - 'Where do you think we should go for our vacation Faith? Let's finalize it now.'

Faith thinks for a while and says - 'Lucy, in the current state, there is mostly water and very little landmass on earth' ... Therefore, why don't we go to a cave for our vacation for 3 days, where we can escape from the landmass, satellite and people around us?'

'Cave for a vacation - are you crazy? Where on earth will you find such a cave?' - Lucy tells Faith in a tone of utter disbelief.

Faith smiles and says- 'There is one such cave which I know exists in a small island that is situated now near the southern part of the landmass. Once upon a time that part of the world used to be known as Mozambique".

'But how do we go there? And more importantly who will take us there?' – In an excited tone, Lucy bombards Faith with questions.

'My dear, don't worry too much now, as we talk, the arrangements are being finalized', Sensing her disbelief, Faith beams and shares the fact with Lucy, 'I have already made a request to the council of Earth this morning without telling you about this vacation as I wanted to give you a surprise'.

'That's really great - I sincerely appreciate the gesture. But did the council approve?' - Lucy eagerly inquires.

'Yes, they've approved my request quite gladly, as Madhyam had strongly recommended it as well', Faith laughs, 'We are crucial members of the earth team after all and helping us to retain our best mental prowess makes perfect sense'.

Barely able to refrain herself from dancing, Lucy exclaims - 'I am really happy. You perfectly understand my subconscious desire. Yes, I am very much looking for a vacation before going for the negotiations'.

In a thoughtful tone, as if talking to herself, Faith utters - ' I understand the subconscious of most humans, that's how I have been groomed and trained'.

'Well, what do you mean by that Faith?' Lucy inquisitively remarks, as the reply sounds slightly out of context to her.

'Perhaps you will understand the meaning of my odd words in coming future. Treat them as gibberish for the time being', Faith says in an absent-minded manner. And immediately after, she smartly changes the topic of their discussion by adding - 'In fact, the council was very happy that I had put up the application. The head of the council of earth feels that this vacation is very important for us to stay fresh and alert during the entire course of negotiations. This is because often during the negotiations we may have to constantly work for more than 24 hours at one stretch.'

Lucy solemnly says - 'Faith, you are my best friend. So when are we going to this place?'

Faith replies - ' The negotiation as far as I know will begin only by end of next week. I met Madhyam this morning, who updated me on this development. The head of the council has arranged a private jet for us to reach the island with the cave. This jet takes only 15 minutes to reach this island as it travels in supersonic speed. There is a special underground resort in that island where we will stay and the necessary arrangements have already been made. Hope my initiative and arrangements have made you happy Lucy'.

Lucy comes running to Faith and hugs her, as she feels that a mere word of gratitude will not be able to express her feelings sufficiently.

Next day, they pack their bags and go to the nearest airport, which is around 1 hour from their residence. As part of the ongoing sustainability initiative, this airport was made in a self-sustained way, and thereby has been completely relying on solar, wind, waste and all other forms of renewable sources to meet its energy demand. Lucy and Faith boards the private jet, which was waiting for them there. It looks like a small elliptical body with a constant whirl of jet coming from the back.

Lucy boards and tells Faith in a conspirational tone - 'It's not too big'.

Faith laughs and says -'What were you expecting?'

Lucy also smiles and says - 'Well I don't know what exact dimensions were in my mind, but that was definitely not this small'!

With an understanding smile in her face, Faith consoles Lucy by rationalizing -' Look onto the content and not the size or dimensions - as the age-old adage says, small is always beautiful'.

The jet takes off and within a short while it reaches the special airport on the land that has a gateway to the cave.

After the 15-minute flight, they gather their luggage and de-board the aircraft. Lucy comes out of the jet and in a cheerful tone tells Faith -'Well I am convinced now that small is indeed sharp and beautiful. And efficient as well'.

As soon as they reach the terminal building, two persons, one man and one woman, come forward and receive them. They introduce themselves as, Liam and Emiko, designated guides for Lucy and Faith during their vacation. Liam and Emiko then escort them towards an elevator in the airport that goes down straight to the entrance of the cave.

Lucy surveys her surroundings with keen interest. The airport in the island did not look like any public airport she has seen earlier and seemed to be made for these special visits only. However, the airport from where they boarded the flight was a public airport in which one side had a dedicated terminal for the special supersonic jets. The normal flights were taking place from another terminal.

She suddenly stops on her track to notice that the board at the top of the gate of the elevator has the following heading -

'Gateway to Artificial Vacation of Hell'.

Lucy gets curious with the unusual choice of words for the heading and enquires from the two guides about the underlying reason.

Liam casually answers - 'Well, going down the earth metaphorically means going to hell - but we have created a vacation spot down there and have imposed a positivity to the notion of hell. So we are trying to reverse the age-old concepts in the new world and are actually trying to say that you all are the privileged people to reach hell which has all positivity of vacation for you'.

Emiko adds with a broad smile, 'To complement the explanation of Liam, I'll call this a reminder to the stark reality that earth is no longer the paradise it once used to be. So why the notion of hell should suffer from the stereotype?'

The frown on her face turning into a grin, Lucy nods -'Yes, I get the irony'.

In the lift Lucy suddenly closes her eyes and feels the pressure of the responsibility on their shoulders. The paradise has indeed been lost. But more importantly, can it be restored before it is too late? Will the earthlings be able to unite against the AIs and win the negotiation?

After crossing through almost 15 floor levels the elevator stops. Lucy feels a little curious and asks -'Are we inside a mine?'

'No, you are inside one of the wonders created by humankind, which you will see over the next couple of days' - informs Emiko.

Little surprised, Lucy asks Faith in a hushed voice -'When did our human race created this place and why is this created'?

With a reassuring smile, Faith tells -'You will know everything eventually, but remember for now that we have come here for a vacation. So don't overwork your mind on too many things - just see and absorb these wonders created within the cave'.

Lucy cannot help noticing that while uttering the word 'created', Faith's voice changed a little. Inwards, she felt a little perplexed,

'What has been created in such a remote place?' But she prefers to wait for those secrets to unfold before her eyes in the next few days.

THE VACATION AND THE ISLAND LAB

Third Week of April 2250

L ucy and Faith are provided two separate rooms in the underground residence block which are completely sanitized and has no pollution, centrally air conditioned with an entertainment jukebox mapping their mental state every hour and providing them with a virtual entertainment game and sports or music, films or books. Whenever they select for an option, the jukebox created a virtual environment of it in the room and Lucy and Faith feel that they are a part of a real scenario which can be in a park or music concert where they are sitting or listening to music. Any of their subconscious wish can be fulfilled by this jukebox by creating a background atmosphere.

Amazed by its functioning the first day, Lucy asks, 'Faith, does this entertainment jukebox mean we now understand every aspect of the human mind?'

Faith, who was observing even the minute details of their rooms with keen interest, shakes her head and answers, 'No Lucy, it isn't. I also came to the same conclusion initially. But then I realized that the jukebox is mapping our emotions also from our body movements and biometric changes. I tried to trick the jukebox in that fashion and once it worked!'

After a pause, Faith continues, 'See your actions are going to be very different if you are depressed and overjoyed. Here the jukebox is also checking that and I'll say, guessing the same with great precision. It will take some more time for the humans to correctly sense human emotion and the functioning of the subconscious mind. I'm also trying to learn the art.'

Lucy thoughtfully asks, 'And what about the AIs? Can they perfectly sense human thought?'

Faith takes a few seconds to respond, as if she is measuring her words before sharing them with Lucy. Then she says, 'They can perfectly predict the behaviour and possible course of action of an average individual. They can correctly predict the choices of the mankind. But if a person happens to be an exception, an outlier guided by different set of values and emotions, then even the AIs may fail to do so.'

During the stay, their food, water and any beverage are provided automatically through a service lift that opens in their room. At night, both of them love to come out of the cave in a special elevator carrying a capsule in it. As soon as it reaches the main surface of the island, the capsule detaches from the elevator and take both of them for a night ride on air over the island and the adjoining sea. Sometime in the morning as well, Lucy and Faith enjoy the same ride, and on those occasions they are accompanied by Liam and Emiko. Often Lucy and Faith go for a swim.

Interestingly, Lucy and Faith observe that Liam and Emiko are extremely friendly with them and love to converse on many things related to the cave, the environment surrounding the island, their funny experiences with the tourists who have visited the island in the past and so on. However, they are quite tight-lipped about their past. Whenever asked about that aspect, they politely change the subject of the conversation. Lucy often expresses her perceptions on this unusual behaviour with Faith, who most of the times explain this by saying, 'Maybe they are extremely private persons and do not want to share their life story with us. Let us respect their decision.'

The days passed fast. On the fifth day on the island, Lucy and Faith get up early and head for breakfast. Liam and Emiko join them and they start having food. As per plans, at around the middle of the day they are supposed to fly back to their home.

Suddenly the mini tablet of Lucy makes a sound, indicating that she has received a message. While having food, Lucy opens the text and see that it has come from Madhyam. It is written in a matter of fact manner that there is a high-tech lab in the island. The council of earth feels that both Lucy and Faith should be visiting the facility for some time before their departure.

Slightly perplexed, Lucy calls Madhyam and asks, 'Hey, why did you not intimate us about the lab before'?

Madhyam briefly explains, 'Lucy, once you visit the lab, the answer will automatically come to you. Besides, we did not want you to discuss this lab with anybody before your visit. Upon your return, we'll discuss this in greater details.' Saying this he disconnects the phone.

Once Liam and Emiko are informed about the plan to visit the lab, they broadly smile and their behaviour makes Lucy think that they were waiting for such a request to come at any point. They silently produce two passes for the lab visit, which will remain valid for three hours from the time of entry.

After completing the unusually silent breakfast from then on, Lucy and Faith move towards the lab escorted by Liam and Emiko. The lab is located in a different part of the island, with its entry totally camouflaged by a natural surroundings. The secrecy of Madhyam's message and the location of the lab makes Lucy and Faith understand that something important is going on there. But despite their expectations, they have no idea about the surprises waiting for them.

The two friends move to the lab which is headed by a scientist and there are three persons helping him, two men and a woman. Seeing the three persons behind the scientist, Lucy whispers to Faith – 'I find them a little expressionless and dozed - Do you feel the same Faith?'

Faith replies – 'Yes you are right. They look somewhat weird'.

Unable to contain her feeling, Lucy tells the scientist in charge of the Lab, a person named Pedro, 'We find this place and the people working here little weird'.

Pedro smiles and replies – 'Come with me and you will see more to quench your inquisitiveness'. He then introduces his three colleagues as Valentina, Akil and Indra.

Pedro leads Lucy and Faith accompanied by the three colleagues into a chamber. Lucy's eyes widen in astonishment after entering there. She sees an assembly line of robots who are resembling humans, though they have machines fitted in their entire body. The robots belong to both the genders in appearances. Greatly perplexed by the view, Lucy asks Pedro – 'What is this?'

Pedro replies, 'These are the future of AIs with all human conscious, subconscious and unconscious layers of mind. They have all complexities of human mind and they understand each and every bit of human feelings. Even Valentina, Akil and Indra are robots of the first successful prototype batch. They help me in fulfilling my duties here.'

Faith suddenly asks, 'If you don't mind, let me ask you something. Do scientists really understand all the aspects of human conscious, subconscious and unconscious layers of mind?'

Pedro grudgingly admitted, 'Well, we have learnt a lot about various dimensions of the human mind and you have seen a good example of that in the residential quarters. And I can assure you that our knowledge on the working of the human mind is improving every day '.

Lucy keeps staring at the three humanoid machines in amazement. They are wonderful creations indeed!

Pedro continues, 'This facility was started by the head of the council of earth and satellite some years back in 2230, with some funding support from satellite. The purpose was to build next generation of AIs with complete human consciousness and soul that can take care of every wish and need of human beings and ensure their prosperity for future. Therefore, whenever you both form a wish in your mind, the three AIs can read it and they were always ready to serve you. I thought before you depart from the island you should see this chamber and the direction in which we are heading'.

Lucy and Faith both feels surprised and also a little worried. Lucy voices her concern, "But, the future possibilities really worry me. I'm not very optimistic about the ulterior motives of the satellite. What if through this research they ever try to make the humanoid AIs to serve them instead of serving humanity, by controlling them in future?'

Pedro dismisses their concern with a wave of his hand, 'Well, as of now it has been a collaborative exercise and any misdirection has never happened.'

With a frown glued to her face, Lucy says slowly – 'But I am not convinced about our future'.

Faith interjects, 'In my opinion we should look at the possibilities with more positivity, Lucy. Imagine the knowledge that we've gained through this research. Had the funding were not extended, this breakthrough would not have been possible.'

Lucy shakes her head and counters, 'I cannot help thinking that the primary beneficiary of the research project are the AIs. Mankind has survived for so many centuries without the knowledge on conscious, subconscious and unconscious minds through this type of a project, they've learnt it through their experience. Now when we are facing a crisis in the form the sustainability and livelihood challenges, was this really a priority matter?'

'Now, who will enjoy the benefits of this project? Of course the AIs. In future during the negotiations, don't you think the AIs would be mapping the emotions of the humans, based on their learnings from this project?'

Faith objects by pointing out, 'You forget Lucy that the AIs have arrived from another galaxy after watching the humans for a very long time. Only when they felt that the humans, on their own, are incapable of course-correction and would continue on the path of inflicting irreversible damage on the environment, they decided to intervene. They already have a fair amount of knowledge on our behavioural pattern and the working of the subconscious mind. You rather focus on the benefits. The humanoid AIs are capable of supplementing the efforts of humans in generating essentials for our livelihood. That's a big help.'

Pedro, who was watching the exchange between Lucy and Faith with a smiling face, answers in an assuring tone, - 'Don't worry on this matter now, Lucy. Just devote your full mind and energy to the upcoming negotiations. It is my job to ensure that the research here stays on the desired course. Why don't you flip through our findings?'

For the next three hours, Lucy and Faith read through the summarized research output records of the lab in their documentation room. Due to paucity of time they cannot read the entire reports, and read only the broad findings. Nevertheless, they get a detailed idea about the direction of the research.

At the end of three hours, which just flew by, Pedro comes back to the room and announces, 'So, it's time for you to leave now. Liam and Emiko are waiting outside the lab to take you to your jet on the island airport'.

Shaking hands with him, Lucy says, 'I'll look forward to hear from you, especially on the directions of the research output, with interest'.

On her way out and the journey to the surface, Lucy is not able to forget what she saw and several scenarios and possibilities of future was relaying on her mind. Sensing her unease, Faith keeps on saying to her – 'Relax'.

They reach the airport fifteen minutes before the scheduled departure time. The flight is almost ready to take off. Lucy and Faith shake hands with Liam and Emiko, and profusely thank them for their support.

Liam smiles and wishes them, 'Good luck for the negotiations'.

Emiko interjects, 'Teach the satellite team how to play chess!!'

Faith laughs, 'sure thing'.

Lucy could not help asking the very question that is preoccupying her thought process since her lab visit. 'Do you ever feel uncomfortable while interacting with the three AIs working there in the lab'?

Liam and Emiko start laughing almost hysterically. Lucy wonders what's so funny with her question. There is surely nothing stupid in her words! Even Faith has a faint smile in her lips.

After a few seconds, Emiko composes herself and explains, 'Lucy, the purpose of keeping us with you for the last three days is a grand success. Once you are back, Madhyam is going to enjoy a hearty laugh. We are both humanoid AIs of the latest design. The council of earth in general and Madhyam in particular wanted to test our ability to assimilate with the humans. Looks like we've passed the test with flying colours!'

Within a short span of time, Lucy feels amazed once again. She would never have guessed!! They are so very human by their behaviour. Too moved by the revelation, she just nods.

Faith on the other hand gives a knowing smile, and says 'I sensed something about you right from the beginning. Good to see the technological achievement'.

In a somewhat odd manner, Liam responds, 'We understand what you mean'.

Before Faith can respond, the flight is announced ready for departure. Lucy and Faith board the same and after a short flight, they reach home.

While the vacation was refreshing, the last day's visit to the lab raised quite a few serious questions on humanity's future in Lucy's mind. On their journey back to their home from the airport she asks Faith, 'Why do you think we are making humanoid AIs'?

Faith thinks for a while. Then she slowly answers, 'Lucy, the humankind's ego is hurt when the AIs from another galaxy force them to abandon the satellite. And at home, hardship is so very common. Given the supremacy of the AIs, humankind has taken their technological support to create AIs for helping them. In the first generation of AIs created here in the island lab, the scientist team could not stand the possibility of staring at robots looking like Lazarus besides them. So, they created robots, who can be distinctly identified as machines, and can be considered as inferior to human beings. Just remember the sight of Valentina, Akil and Indra. I feel that the uses of the AIs for various purposes would be growing. But our anger on the satellite AIs is growing. So, now we want to completely forget that they are machines. As a result, Liam and Emiko now look like perfect humans'.

Lucy is still unhappy, 'You mean they'll soon be moving around in our world? And we'll have no means to know whether they are humans or AIs'?

Faith nods, 'In all probability yes. Maybe not tomorrow, but perhaps two years down the line. You see, the council of earth have not shared the news of their existence with the citizens yet. This clearly underlines their hesitation. Moreover, with the anti-AI sentiment at the peak at present, they may think that the news may now hurt them politically. Perhaps they are looking for an opportune moment. Maybe they'll allow the earth-made AIs to roam in all parts of the globe, if we manage to win the negotiation.'

Lucy sighs, 'But will they always remain faithful to us? The AI technology and know-how, originally invented and standardized in another universe, has been used during their construction. Will they not be serving them instead?'

In a thoughtful voice Faith replies, 'Lucy, AIs are guided by logic. Humans are often impulsive and hence they sometimes find the AI action, which is always guided by reason, unjustifiable. But I can assure you that the AIs reciprocate their feeling, as they often fail to understand the logic behind human actions. The earth scientists have seen to this aspect during their research. I do not think the AIs constructed in the island lab will be entirely conditioned by the satellite AI's standpoint. But of course future is uncertain and may hold unexpected outcomes.'

The unexpected ending of the tour and the exposure to the lab is too much for Lucy to grasp. She now feels exhausted and needs a deep sleep to start a new day for the call for negotiations.

However during the sleep that night, during a series of wild dreams Lucy sees that Pedro is an AI spy, who has been sent from the satellite to control the future generation of humanity and also have a control over the thought process of human beings. That night, Lucy wakes up several times from the sleep with a jolt as a result of these nightmares. However, towards the end of the night she is finally embraced by a deep slumber and gets up next morning, eagerly looking forward to upcoming negotiations.

THE NEGOTIATION VENUE

First Week of June 2250

*A*midst *Lucy's wait, preparations to arrange the venue for the negotiation begins in full swing. The councils of earth and satellite prepare for every possible security aspects with minute detail. Apart from the chief representative leaders of different class of societies in earth and the smart cities on earth, representatives from the satellite also intend to attend the event.* The council members, elected by their people, were coded by the AIs of the satellite and the head council of earth for security purposes. Once they get coded, they receive an access card and code to enter negotiation venue in the ship.

In the meantime, the security preparation in the ship reaches its peak as the negotiation organizing committee fears some protest demonstrations by various groups from earth against the AIs from satellite in the ship. So the level of caution in the ship intensifies. In the build up to the security arrangements, special security troops comprising of AIs capable of understanding human emotions, produced at the island lab, with special defence skills are deployed. In addition, security troops nominated by the head council of earth, equipped with special gear, are also posted there. Lucy and Faith hear all these from news broadcasts every day and wait for their call with growing expectations.

Lucy realizes that in tensed times, probability of acceptance for unusual things go up. During normal period, humans would always have objected to deployment of AI troops capable of understanding human emotions, even if they are developed on the earth. But now that the entire focus is on negotiations, and the possibility of defeat and settlement of AIs on earth being discussed everywhere, the council of earth cleverly announces the news with careful choice of words. The announcement rather gave confidence to humans that the earth-made AIs can be a good match to alien AIs in case of any emergency.

Finally one day they receive their negotiation kit with all access cards, travel itinerary and special tickets of a small supersonic round plane for landing on the designated landing zone of the ship.

After five days, Lucy and Faith board the plane. After a short and uneventful journey, they reach the landing zone of the ship. After coming out from the plane, Lucy and Faith are guided by security guards, which are humanoid AIs, to their commanding officer.

Lucy and Faith are informed by the chief security officer about their cabin room number and its location. Soothing light music sounds can be heard all around the deck. Lucy is astonished with the entire arrangement and exclaims to Faith – 'Faith, this place is so well decorated and aptly prepared for the event. I mean, the deck is displaying symbols of regions that are participating in this negotiation. In the notice board of the deck itself, the agenda of all the sessions of the event is given. But I hope, somebody will give us an orientation of this big giant of a ship, as we need to know where each of these venues of the agenda are'.

Faith answers in an assuring tone – 'Well, I know you are getting impatient. I am certain that we will be receiving an orientation today itself'.

Lucy and Faith are accompanied by two security guards to their cabin. After reaching their cabin, the guards hand over their cabin room keys. Lucy and Faith are given two separate cabins and Lucy expresses her disappointment with that, as staying alone in such a big ship makes her slightly nervous. Sensing her fear, Faith reassures Lucy – 'Don't worry, I am staying next door only. If you need me for anything, just call me'.

As the security guards depart, Lucy and Faith enter their two worlds of surprises. The cabins seem nothing less than the rooms of luxurious residences in the smart islands that both have heard about, but never got an opportunity to witness first hand. The cabins are full of amenities, lavish but recyclable toilets and everything that one can expect in a luxurious apartment. But what makes Lucy amazed is the fact that while all the food products placed there are a result of organic farming, all the other products also happen to be bio-degradable in nature. She starts checking all the items once again and this time realizes, while the room in first glance conveys a sense of luxury, it actually is an aesthetic arrangement of normal and sustainable products. She is utterly impressed.

Lucy did not expect to stay in such a lavish, yet sustainable, atmosphere. However, after the brief moments of pleasant surprise, she notices that just beside her bed, there is a complete itinerary, including direction of the various venues on the ship with a GIS gadget.

In the instruction document placed beside the bed, the directives for using the GIS gadget is clearly laid out. The gadget is a very miniature form of a smart phone where in the desktop all the venues of the ship and major locations are kept as icons. The phone is as small as a visiting card and if one speaks the name of the venue in front of the voice receiver of the phone, the gadget map opens up on the screen and it starts showing direction of the intended destination.

The agenda and itinerary also mentions the location of the food court where breakfast, lunch, dinner etc. are being served and how they have to reach these places using the gadget. Breakfast, lunch and dinner start every day from 7.30 a.m., 1.00 p.m. and 8.30 p.m. onwards respectively. The time to enjoy food on all three occasions is one hour each. After these breaks, the participants have to join the negotiations which will stretch for most of the days for a very long time. The documents also explain that for certain days it can continue even for the entire day and night, depending on the context of the negotiation discussions.

Lucy and Faith go through the entire package detailing various aspects of the agenda and itinerary. They proceed together for lunch at 1.00 p.m. to the food court area of the ship adjoining the deck. The food court area has a buffet arrangement with both long rectangular tables as well as short round tables. Lucy and Faith first take their food from the counter and then sit in one corner of a long table while waiting for others.

Gradually they are joined by others and a casual conversation starts between them while having lunch. Lucy and Faith sit together and soon Eman and Ivan comes to the table with their plates.

Lucy courteously greets them and says, 'I suddenly realize that we've not known you at all as a person. All the time we've spent together so far has gone towards cognitive and non-cognitive parts of human brain, AI programming language and of course the Protocol! Tell me something about you'.

Eman jokes – 'Can I just say, "Hi, I am Eman"'?

Faith laughs and says, 'I think Lucy wants you to start from the next line'.

All of them laugh at her witty remark and Eman then starts, 'Well, me and my ancestors belonged to Satellite. My father's name was Emanuel'.

Hearing the name, suddenly Lucy thinks and remembers that she had long back met a person named Emanuel in the train in the ice age. But surely that must have been in a dream that she had and not in the reality of actual events!! Yet, it seems so real! Lucy cannot figure the boundary where the dream ends and reality begins!!!

Sensing her preoccupation in a train of thought, Eman asks Lucy – 'Why are you so lost suddenly'?

With some hesitation, Lucy replies, 'I think I might have met a namesake of your father in my dream'.

Eman gets startled and asks – 'How come'?

Lucy answers back – 'I don't know how, but I am quite convinced of meeting him in my dream, when I boarded in a train during 2150'.

Slightly perplexed, Eman continues, 'My dad was a resident of the Satellite and he participated in a movement against the AI's ill-intent of controlling the growth prospect of humanity. Then he was trapped in an environmental scam regarding a housing construction in the Satellite. Apparently dad used to tell me that the AI chief of the Satellite council put his name in the scam just on the basis of circumstantial evidence and sent him back to Earth by demeaning his image so that the movement my dad was leading against the AI of the council can be stopped. He never did anything to damage the environment, but merely knew some people who were involved in that scam. I was born here when he came back. My mom and dad met each other at the smart island, after his return from the Satellite. He became one of the leading members of our council on earth and was always vocal against the AIs. With the climate disaster intensifying and the earth largely getting submerged in water, my dad lost my mother while making a relocation to a safe land. Then he decided to be a part of the climate movement against the AIs and strive for a negotiation where humans and AI can negotiate on a protocol and take responsibility of their actions causing climate change.'

Eman closes his eyes for a few seconds, and continues after a few seconds' silence, 'He also started a small climate activism group against the AIs. Gradually, more council leaders embraced the idea of promoting green activities and such voices started gaining a prominence in different councils of various income classes on earth. My dad recently died due to health ailments, but his movement did not stop and today we are here in this negotiation platform. I was truly impressed by meeting Madhyam here, who along with Jack and Bruke, brought together several representatives from various walks of life from the middle income class of earth.'

Lucy and Faith answer in the affirmative. They concentrate on the food for some time. Lucy silently wonders, 'was it really Eman's father that she met in the train? Or Emanuel was just a projection in her dream, whose name coincidentally matches with the name of Eman's father?'

Discussions with Eman enabled Lucy to comprehend the scale of the negotiation movement and also the nature of convergence of their stories. She feels that her story, life journey and Eman's one has a commonality of the fight against the AIs. 'But why did I meet Emanuel in the earlier dream?' Lucy is still not clear about the answer. Irritated, she promises herself to figure the answer out some day.

Suddenly, a voice resonates in Lucy's mind. She feels as if her dad is telling her about Emanuel – 'Emanuel is my coding character in the train, my child, and you are there too'. It feels so much like her own father's voice!

She muses whether this means her father was experimenting with the subconscious projection of her mind, which led to the train experience and her encounter with those characters is still preserved in her mind as dreams. But how can that be possible? She has not met her father since gaining consciousness.

Lucy comes out of her thoughts and concentrates on the food, as suddenly Faith interjects in a concerned voice – 'My dear friend when will you eat?'

But Lucy instead asks Ivan, 'And what about you?'

Ivan lets out a dry chuckle. 'I'm afraid my story is hardly as interesting as that of Eman. My relatives have never defied gravity and left the earth's crust. Ever.'

'We used to reside in a small hamlet in a faraway island. Only a few families used to stay there as the limited resources and fragile environment was not enough to support more people. But once the melting of ice led to rise in sea level, our existence faced a serious threat.'

'We feared death as it was not possible to cross the ocean in our small fishing boats to reach the landmass. But fortunately a ship came to our rescue after a month and took us to the landmass. It arrived in time, our island by that time shrank to one-third of its original size. And we were already starving. But bigger challenges awaited us in the climate refugee colony.'

'You see, in the island we were working day-and-night for food but were fiercely independent. We never felt poverty because all of us were on a similar level of material possession.'

'But in the climate refugee colony, we were offered the most barren and land-locked region to live. The middle-income group had already taken possession of the coastal regions. So, overnight our most efficient fishermen became jobless, just another unskilled labour, at his wit's end, to survive in a dry landmass.'

'In the island, there was a natural birth rate and environmental adjustment. But here people from various faraway places were rescued and put in a hostile and unknown territory and left to their fate for survival. Given the limited resources, opportunities shrank and demand abound. The leadership of the climate refugee groups tried to negotiate with the elites and the middle-income groups for improving our lot. Aids came, but that was way below the required level. Politicians and bureaucrats flourished as they distributed favours. Who bothers to think about a common man? So, malnutrition and consequent death followed.'

Ivan closes his eyes, as if he is living those painful memories once again. Everybody remain silent, unsure of what to say.

Finally, Faith gently asks, 'How did you reach here?'

Ivan laughs in a lifeless manner. 'Well, after Bruke became the leader of our colony, the scenario marginally improved. He persuaded the elites and the middle-income groups to invest in our localities, as the labour cost is cheaper. So, with that development some improvement in lifestyle was noticed. Subsequently the elites organized an exam for finding talents and I scored a high grade there. So, I was given a scholarship to come to the smart islands to study for the next ten years.'

Lucy asks, 'That must have been a really coveted opportunity?'

Ivan sighs, 'Yes and no. You see, my parents were dead by that time. They could never adjust to the landlocked lifestyle that persisted in the neighbourhood. They missed the ocean dearly. I just wanted to leave the land behind. So, I think my desire to leave the climate refugee colony was stronger than the attraction of the smart cities.'

Eman intervenes, 'But, you later returned to the place!'

Ivan responds after a while, 'Yes. Once my studies were over, I somehow started feeling an urge to face my life, not run away from it. See, I was among the toppers in my class. I had to be..., there was no other preoccupation for me, ... there was no family or any other distraction. But outside my classroom, I was still considered only as an immigrant in the smart cities. Sometime, people would air their contempt, sometimes they would let you know their mind through unspoken behaviour or careful choice of words. So, I decided to come back to the climate refugee colony and lend my support to Bruke in his endeavours.'

Lucy realizes the common bond between the four of them. All have lost their families at relatively young ages and took that as a challenge – that they have to prove their worth to the world. Perhaps that's the reason behind their success in life so far.

Faith says, 'I'm so sorry to hear about your losses. It's good to have a person like you in the team'.

Ivan laughs and then adds with a sudden outburst of passion, 'I volunteered for this. You see, I lost my home, the small hamlet in the inconsequential island, once. I do not want to lose my home, the *earth* this time, to the AIs. This is not just a negotiation for me, I consider this as a mission of my life'.

After a few minutes of silence, Eman asks Lucy and Faith, 'Well, anything to share from your side '?

Before Lucy opens her mouth, Faith answers, 'Well, we also lost our near and dear ones early and tried to find solace in our studies. But one thing I would like to add here. The smart cities developed, expanded with relocation possibility to satellite and shrank again with appearance of the alien AIs. The climate refugee colony faced extreme hardship. In that comparison, our territory neither developed that sharply, nor did disappointing scenarios emerged. In that sense, life for us was less stressful.'

Lucy senses that Faith does not want to share intimate details, perhaps given her early losses. So she refrains from adding further comments.

Afterwards Lucy and Faith complete the lunch silently. Then they say bye to Eman and Ivan and head towards the cabin as in the evening they are supposed to get briefed on the long-awaited negotiations that starts tomorrow.

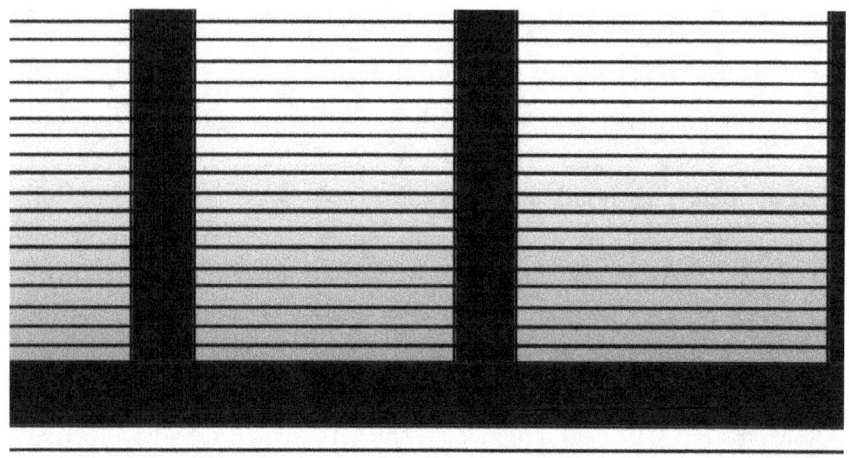

THE EVENING BRIEFING

In the evening at 6.00 p.m. a briefing session is organized in one of the lecture halls of the ship. Donald, Head of the Protocol Secretariat, jointly developed by humans and AIs for the negotiations, arranges the event with his team. Donald, a resident of the smart islands, is wearing a black spectacle and a tailor-made black suit. A middle-aged woman accompanies him, but Lucy cannot relate her to any particular group. Seeing her the only person who comes on Lucy's mind is Indra, the AI prototyped human being she saw in the vacation outing with Faith.

There is a small stage in the hall, which has five chairs. After a few minutes, once everyone is settled, the briefing session begins. Donald and the lady Lucy noticed, goes to the stage. The lady was introduced by Donald as Iris, an AI from the satellite.

The briefing starts in a very organized manner and it seems that the two representatives know exactly what to say with a precise sense of timing. Their first point of the briefing starts with the definition of a chess game that will be played between the council representatives of earth and satellite. Each representative of the various income classes of earth are required to unite to form a single chess team and then they will play a game of chess against the representatives from satellite, who are humanoid AI prototypes with understanding of the deep subconscious of human mind.

It is evident from the narration that, the AIs will be aware of the human thought process and strategic moves in the game of chess. Therefore it is required that somebody present in the Earth chess team also understands the core of the AI prototyped human' mind.

Suddenly, Lucy realizes why her presence is indispensable in the Earth council team, as was mentioned by Madhyam and their trainers to her earlier. She also realizes why the vacation to the island was not a 'vacation' in the true sense, as the visit to the AI lab and interactions with Liam and Emiko and Valentina, Akil and Indra, i.e., humanoid AIs of various batches, was a crucial step to prepare her for this moment.

Donald goes on further – 'There will be three games of chess. Whoever will win the series can impose an act of mitigation and adaptation on the losing side. The action will be to construct a green, energy efficient residential complex for the winners in the habitat of the losers. Essentially, this means, if the earth chess team loses the game, then the satellite team will impose a commitment on Earth to construct green, energy efficient residential space on Earth so that more AIs from the satellite can come and stay there. As residents of the planet, they'll have greater rights to influence earth's sustainability actions. If the AI team loses, they have to offer a similar concession in satellite for the earth inhabitants. So, the humans can resettle in the satellite, provided they embrace the sustainability practices. And if it's a draw then the status quo persists. N'Cono and Raghav will be the two players representing earth and satellite respectively.'

Lucy can immediately foresee the future – 'A loss for the earth team will mean more AI control in the councils of the earth with more space for AIs on our planet. This will mean a gradual loss of control to AI'. With rising water level on the earth, if more and more humans get the opportunity to live on the satellite that augments the survival potential of the species. But if the AIs come for living here, then the resulting shrink of the living space may lead to mankind's further marginalization and even extinction in long run. This is something, she cannot let happen.

Taking a deep breath, Lucy mutters to herself – 'I have to help our team and can't allow such a grim scenario to evolve - A World with Extinction of Humanity and Human Intelligence substituted by Artificial Intelligence'.

Her thought process is interrupted by the continued speech of the Secretariat representative. Donald further adds – 'We expect at least 2500 strategic moves will be exercised by both sides in each of the chess games. But the moves of this game will be sequential and will be in response to each other in an iterative way. So you all will be exposed to the best of strategic thinking and move prediction abilities by means of the chess games'.

'If the two sides agree, then the games may go on for 24 hours without any disturbance. But if the teams agree to have a recess, that will follow.'

'And of course, once the three games are over, with the result in hand, the council of the satellite will sit with the council of earth to discuss the details of the compliance.'

'The next part of the briefing deals with your venue, dress codes and all other logistics' – Donald completes his sentence. Iris comes to the stage and in a business-like precision shares the relevant information to everybody.

Once the announcement is over, Iris leaves the stage. Donald, who stays on the stage, now invites the others there. Lazarus, Jack, Raghav and N'Cono comes forward and occupies the remaining chairs.

Donald first asks Lazarus to share his views. Lazarus gives a short speech for a few minutes, ending with, 'I'm sure that the negotiation will result in the victory of the side using the mental prowess most logically, so that the principle of sustainable development can flourish further.' and several other representatives from the council of AIs silently nods.

The speech of Lazarus is followed by a passionate speech by Jack, the leader of the elites, who starts with, 'Granted that the mankind made certain wrong choices, but can there be no chance for redemption?' he then goes on to recount all the steps taken in the earth to ensure environmental sustainability over the last decade, and ends with, 'We are here to win the game of chess, the following negotiation and ultimately our rightful place in the satellite. Let this win mark the victory of natural intellect over AIs'. The speech receives cheerful applause from the representatives of all the three income groups of earth.

Donald then invites Raghav to say a few words. Raghav gets up and speaks clearly about the mission of the AIs, i.e., the need to protect the environment, the habitable planets and the importance of having an AI settlement on earth, as a result of winning the chess game, to further these goals. His speech, outlining their vision for the protocol, receives a silent admiration from the AI team.

Finally, N'Cono gets up and starts with a wary smile on his face, 'Well, I have very little to add. We the earthmen are here today, as a team, to negotiate with the AIs. The team consists of brilliant minds from all parts of the earth, our home. I sincerely wish that in the past we had worked with such solidarity, which would surely have caused a course correction and spared us from seeing this day. Today we are negotiating with invaders to our planet, and a defeat might compromise our right to stay in our own planet. Satire indeed!!' He stops and wipes the sweat from his forehead.

'Today, our team is not from *Eden, Domus* or *the Reef*, but represent the Earth. And I'm sure we'll be representing *Elios* soon.'

There is pin-drop silence in the room now.

After a few moments, N'Cono continues in his passionate voice, 'So, we have a huge responsibility on our shoulder. I sincerely hope that the collective wisdom of our Earth team will be able to outperform the intellect of the AI delegation. We HAVE TO, because defeat is not an option for us anymore.' He abruptly stops and goes back to his chair.

It takes a few seconds for everybody to understand that his speech is over. Then the representatives from earth clap for a full minute. N'Cono has just aptly summarized what is resonating in everybody's mind. Lucy spots Eman, Ivan and several other persons standing up and shouting words of approval.

The AIs on the other hand sit with tight lips and hardened expressions. It is clear that N'Cono has conveyed his point home, and the significance of calling them 'invaders' has not been lost on the AIs.

Lazarus, Jack, Raghav and N'Cono now come down from the stage and Iris goes there to join Donald. Although Donald is now talking on how to take the results of the negotiations forward, Lucy does not listen to the briefing anymore and starts looking for Madhyam in the hall. Towards the end of the briefing session she locates Madhyam in one of the middle rows. Lucy motions him to come towards the rear side of the room, and once they are within earshot says – 'I am happy that you put me in the non-playing team that will be advising the leader of the playing team to make the moves'.

Madhyam laughs – 'I am also happy that both you and Faith are in our team. Come to the negotiation hall tomorrow by 6 a.m. and also get Faith along'.

Lucy nods and stands near the rear wall to listen to the remaining part of Donald's brief, which continues for another ten minutes. She realizes that from a distance the content is becoming clearer for her to comprehend. Lucy grasps that, philosophically, a certain degree of aloofness from a particular scenario is better for understanding the wider context.

Finally, at the end of the speech, the structure of the chess game gets a little clearer to Lucy. It will involve two people who will play the game - one from earth and one from satellite, i.e., N'Cono and Raghav. But each one will be accompanied by a big team of advisors who will constantly calculate the future possible moves of the opponent and advise the player. So the non-playing team will also play a crucial role.

The earth advisory team will be comprised of noted individuals, representatives from different income classes of earth and Lucy is one of them. Similarly, the Satellite chess representative will also have an advisory team.

With a deeper understanding on the game, Lucy tells herself – 'So, I have to understand the strategic mind and all possible future moves that can form within the mind of the AI beings. Now I understand why Faith and I went through the interactions with AIs in the island lab'.

The gathered crowd slowly disperses after the end of the session and Lucy sees Faith coming slowly towards her. Once they are together, Lucy asks Faith in an excited tone – 'Where were you in the hall, I could not see you?'

Faith answers – 'I was very much in the hall and listened to everything with interest. I also overheard the discussion between Madhyam and yourself. Let us be there in the negotiation hall by 6 a.m. tomorrow.'

'Bravo, can't wait for tomorrow to come' - Lucy exclaims in an excited tone.

That night Lucy could not sleep for quite some time, as the lunch-time conversations were still resonating in her head. She always associated the smart island elites and climate refugees with happiness and hardship respectively. The narrations of Eman and Ivan today changed her perception. Now she realises that one cannot stereotype any group of people. Various possibilities in the future, resulting from negotiation outcomes, keep playing in her mind. Finally she sleeps, dreaming that the AIs have agreed to return to their planet, taking the AIs created in island lab along with them.

BEGINNING OF THE GAME

Lucy and Faith arrives at the negotiation hall at 6 a.m., the next day. Madhyam greets both of them and says – 'Come, let me show you the codes of the moves. You have to remember certain important strategic moves that we have stored in a chip, which will be injected under the skin of your hand. This is a compilation of at least 5000 strategic moves that an AI brain can make in a game of chess. My hunch is they might come handy during the game'.

Faith suddenly asks Madhyam – 'How on Earth we compiled this?'

Madhyam responds – 'It has been a 20 year long project, initiated when our ancestors were expelled from satellite. Shortly after that we started building this archive of all strategic moves of AI prototyped humans. Our ancestors tried to think like the AIs and correctly reasoned that, in a future date, they may offer to conduct the negotiation, based on the results of a chess game.'

Lucy asks incredulously, 'How can they be so sure?'

Madhyam laughs heartily and says, 'We were NOT sure about anything. In fact, we prepared anticipating AI inclination for a few alternate modes of negotiations as well, and equipped ourselves along those lines too. Maybe those contingencies will come to our aid someday in future, if the AIs do not drastically change their thought process.'

Faith says in an almost inaudible voice, 'Interesting'.

Madhyam pauses for a few seconds and continues thoughtfully, 'It came to our knowledge that, the AIs are also doing something to keep their spies on earth in various locations and preparing themselves for the negotiation. So we had to keep our initiative totally secret. We programmed and preserved the moves in a small chip, which we will embed under your skin. The chip can easily permeate through human skin automatically and so you won't feel any pain. Please extend your hands'.

Lucy and Faith stretches their hand forward and the chip is put inside their hands beneath their skin through a device. Madhyam solemnly adds, 'Only the brains of you two will be able to process the information in the chip and it will help our chess moves to win over the representative of satellite. Then we can impose the responsibility on the satellite inhabitants to accommodate us there in a green and energy efficient space.'

Lucy and Faith cheer jubilantly – 'This is great'.

Madhyam stops them with a serious expression in his face and says – 'Don't you think it's too early to celebrate? Now go back to your rooms to relax a bit and come back here by 10 a.m. The chess game starts then and we need to win for the sake of humanity'.

Faith and Lucy takes their breakfast and arrives in the negotiation hall at the designated hour. The negotiation hall has a big stage which has flags depicting the councils of earth and satellite at the two ends. The stage also has two big tables and at least twelve chairs. There is one chair which is kept in front of two tables, but a little separated from the other chairs. So, it is clear that there are two players who will play and execute the moves on the chessboard on the table and they will be accompanied by at least twelve supporting team mates.

There is an electronic display of the chessboard on the big screen so that the entire hall can see the chess moves. Also, all the chess moves is going to be displayed on the giant screen. The declaration after every move will be shown on the screen. For announcement of recess, break or any other events, there are two women who sat in one corner of the room. Their job is to coordinate and make important announcements for spectators. If a game is won or lost, the outcome and negotiation discussions and decisions which will happen on the table will also be communicated by these two announcers. Outcomes and proceedings of negotiations on the stage are being communicated to these two women by two officials on stage who are constantly communicating the updates and also facilitating the display on the giant screen through their electronic gadgets.

Lucy notes from the logistic details of the programme circulated to all participants mentions that the negotiation related chess games will run for 5 days. The expectation is that the three chess game series will be over in five days. The chess games can run for 24 hours, if the players feel like playing without a recess.

First day of the negotiation starts with a speech from the earth and satellite secretariat representatives, Madhyam and Barbara. Madhyam describes the historical journey of why the negotiation day has arrived and the importance of the negotiation to decide on the future of humanity and a mutual coexistence between humans and AI. In her speech, Barbara becomes quite vociferous about the need for a successful implementation of the Protocol in this juncture to decide the fate of satellite and earth. After almost a 30 minute speech by the two representatives followed by a continuous clamouring and clapping by all spectators, the first chess game began.

Lucy observes that each main chess player, Raghav and N'Cono, has a time keeper beside them. Behind the representative from earth, the non-playing team comprising of individuals from all income classes of the earth took their seats. It includes Lucy and Faith too. The viewers are seated in the gallery. Through a toss, it was decided that the satellite is going to take the white pieces. The first game moves proceed slowly with each moves by the players often taking even thirty minutes. It becomes a game of patience. Moreover, the main chess players are also consulting their respective non-playing teams, which made the game slower. Lucy and Faith, along with Eman and Ivan, contribute from time to time in the thought process of the earth non-playing team regarding the next and the subsequent moves from their side.

The day passes slowly as if everything is moving in a slow motion. In between like a routine, lunch, tea break and dinner sessions are organized. No conclusion to the game is reached and around 4 a.m. the game moderator announces a recess for a few hours. The two chess players take a break and moves towards their own cabin for some rest. The negotiation began on a Monday and till Tuesday there was no decision of the first game.

Tuesday, at 10 a.m. everybody gathers back again in the negotiation hall for the continuation of the first chess game. After almost three hours of cold and patient strategic fight, the first check call comes from satellite for earth. In the next one hour, the earth team dodges attacks of the satellite team and finally at the end of the one hour, they manage to check satellite team!!

After the first check, the earth team constantly attacks satellite. By end of Tuesday, earth team wins the first game and demands settlement of humans in one of the energy efficient green building space of the satellite. The entire food court during dinner on Tuesday gets filled up with the sound of jubilant victory songs where each council representative of earth express happiness according to their customs. On the other hand, an environment of melancholic calm looms over the Satellite camp.

In the backdrop of jubilant singing and cheering from the earth quarters around, Lucy and Faith go to have dinner together.

During dinner-time conversations, Lucy suddenly asks, 'It seems from the expression that the AIs are unhappy. I always thought that they rely on logic and never feel sad. That emotion is perhaps too illogical for them. What do you feel?'

Faith thinks for a while and answers, 'Well, the AIs are staying for too long with the humans now. Perhaps they are acquiring more humane qualities than they can either fathom or are willing to openly accept. That's all I can think to justify their expression.'

Lucy finds a strange expression on Faith's face. 'Are you unhappy for some reason, Faith?' – She asks, in a slightly perplexed tone.

'Well, let me assure you, I am quite happy' - replies Faith, in an absent- minded manner.

Lucy is not entirely convinced with this reply and in a bemused state of mind, both of them head towards their cabin. The sound, music, celebration gradually becomes milder as they move away from the dining hall to the residence quarters of the ship.

THIRD DAY NEGOTIATION LUNCH

The chess game of Wednesday begins with a bang for the Earth team. From the very first move, the satellite team creates a storm of attack, with the clear goal of snatching victory. Each time before a defense can be erected by the earth team, newer set of attacks are launched by the satellite team. The desperate defense continues till lunchtime and finally just when the spectators are waiting for the lunch bell as a rescuer of the earth team, they are checkmated.

As a negotiation move, the earth loses the green energy efficient building spaces it gained in the satellite by winning the first game. Rather it now faces a challenge of allowing habitation by AIs of satellite on the earth. With the overall result now evenly balanced, the third game becomes a decider for the negotiation outcome. Over the next two and half days, the third and final game will be fought, deciding the future of humanity and AIs. With a tense, excited, forward looking frame of mind, the players, team members, spectators and all participants in the ship move towards the lunch hall on Wednesday.

In the table of the lunch hall, Madhyam and Bruke sit together and through conversations, they discover that both have lost their near relatives due to the climate disasters in their respective habitats. The discussions help both to realize that they are sharing a common cause and mission of fighting against the AIs, so that the satellite can be made to concede living quarters to the humans again through the protocol.

Traditionally, the three councils on earth always view the actions of each other with certain degree of suspicion. The elites

111

in *Eden* always believe in their supremacy, given their technological and intellectual edge. They are not willing to even accommodate many people from *Domus* or *the Reef* in their territories. They also consider the practices followed by the other two income groups environmentally non-sustainable, which is the primary reason behind their decision to never support the demand from the resident of *Domus* or *the Reef* for relocation right to the satellite.

The climate refugees the *Reef*, with limited technological achievements and a more basic education pattern, on the other hand always find that the resident of *Eden* and *Domus* are unwilling to share technical know-how with them. The council of *Domus*, which attempts to maintain a balance in their education system on both natural as well as social science, has a better understanding of the psyche of the other two regions and can rationalize their actions more dispassionately. However, self-interest has often forced them to adopt tough negotiating positions against both the neighbours in the past. As a result, mutual mistrust often is the first reaction at the council of earth when any one region tables a proposal on climate change.

But today, with the impending possibility of defeat in the hands of the AIs, suddenly Madhyam and Bruke realizes that coming to a mutually agreeable solution to the environmental challenges facing the earth is after all not so difficult and is desirable in the interest of all the income groups! In the course of their long discussion during lunch, Madhyam and Bruke passionately discusses how they plan to bring new proposals for implementing on earth and satellite if the earth team wins the chess game series. These future proposals would pertain to protect people of all income groups from growing waste volumes, create new green infrastructures, manage disproportionate use of space and so on. Their discussions also relate to various aspects of collective conservation of the planet's resources for humanity, life and channelization of them to people's benefits and not for money and power. They further agree that resource capping of renewables should also be a prominent feature of the joint set of agenda for implementation in earth.

Jack, equally worried with the possibility of defeat in the negotiations, joins them at the lunch table. He knows clearly in his heart that if the AIs come for settlement on the earth as a result of their win, they will target the *Eden*, for the simple reason that most of the green settlements are located therein. This would simply lead to a rise in population therein and possibly street fights in the smart islands, where people are already angry with the AI actions. With stakes so high, he realizes that there is no option for them but to join hands with other income groups and forget all the internal differences dividing the human race.

Though initially he was reserved in his opinions, towards the end of the luncheon discussions, he agrees with the other two in principle. Nevertheless, he points to the other two that as the *Domus* and *the Reef* are lagging behind in creation of green settlements within their territories, they should expand their efforts in this regard without delay.

Bruke gets angry by Jack's unkind remark and snaps back, 'Today you are complaining against our lack of green settlements! For how long have we requested for aids in the form of technical know-how for just supporting the environmental balance in *the Reef*? Rising population and lack of technology has simply increased poverty there. For a long time we have stressed that in our place without sufficient opportunities for earning livelihood, pressure on vulnerable resources is increasing! Have you ever helped us on that?'

Jack replies somewhat stiffly, 'But in *Eden*, with so many people returning from *Elios*, population pressure has increased as well. We are trying our level best to keep the environmental balance intact there.'

Bruke retorts, 'You are forgetting that they returned from *Elios* with some AI technology as well. And the benefit was shared by all the residents of Eden'.

Jack counters, 'We have provided scholarships to a number of *the Reef* residents. In fact today I spotted one of those persons in the negotiating team as well. Are these measures not a support, underlining our positive intent?'

Bruke snaps back, 'NO. That is pure economics.... You brought in young talented students and turned them into professionals, employing them by paying throughway remunerations. That measure is helpful for developing your economy. But they remained outsiders in your smart islands. How many of these people got residency permissions in Eden?'

Jack remains silent and shifts uneasily in his chair.

Sensing the growing anger of Bruke, Madhyam who is always level-headed, now intervenes, 'Friends, today is the least appropriate day for a quarrel among ourselves.'

'Bruke, to defeat the AIs and to break the embrace of gravity, the support of Jack and his team is crucial. Remember because the people from *Eden* built the satellite in 2180, today we are here for the negotiations. Otherwise, we might have been fighting over the limited resources available in the planet.'

'And Jack, if even today we continue to de-link development and environment, then we've failed to learn anything from climate change discussions during Twentieth and Twenty-first centuries. We must complement each other's' journey towards sustainability.'

The wise words on Madhyam brings the discussion back on track. While they are discussing the possible course of sustainable actions in future, a person silently comes and sits beside them. After listening for some time, he suddenly intervenes by saying – 'Sorry, after listening to your discussions, I realized that my great grandfather also used to mention these proposals. I'll say that they have emerged from his lineage. Today, we are again discussing the same set of actions. Does this mean that during the earlier days also people were expecting a climate crisis and therefore thinking of these proposals and just passing the thought to their descendants?'

Even before Jack, Madhyam or Bruke can say anything, the unknown person leaves the table and disappears amongst the surrounding crowd. It seemed like a ghost from the past came and took them to the past in a time machine. As the earth council had stored all the previous times data and research works in a time vault, they have learnt about the lives, works and philosophy of many dignitaries of the past centuries. The person, offering this unexpected counsel and afterwards disappearing like a ghost, has an uncanny resemblance with Nicola Tesla, whose life and works are well known to many people. It appears that Tesla wanted to communicate that – 'We have to care more for renewables, resources, humanity and not for money and that's what pure science stood for'.

Still surprised, Jack, Madhyam and Bruke complete their lunch and quickly head towards the negotiation hall after encountering the mystic, surreal appearance of the man resembling Tesla and his magical disappearance.

Post lunch, the third and final game begins. The day passes by through cautious set of moves by both earth and satellite teams, as no side is willing to suffer a loss this time. Around 7 p.m. both players decide to take a break for the day and start the final game next day by 8 a.m. The tea breaks become short and the activities of the day ends soon.

As Lucy and Faith rise from their chairs to depart from the hall along with others from the negotiation hall, an announcement is made – 'Today, we have an early dinner followed by a cultural night for two hours. So, please enjoy the festivity of earth and satellite after dinner'.

Surprised, Lucy asks Faith, 'Will the AIs enjoy the cultural performances, when they are looking for a victory in negotiations? Won't a song be a distraction for them in the current settings?'

Faith laughs, 'Maybe not, Lucy. Perhaps, they'll find the flawless pattern of a symphony logical and therefore stimulating.'

Lucy cannot but agree to this view.

Exhausted by the day's engaging schedule, Lucy does not want to attend the cultural evening as she wants to sleep early. Faith on the other hand wants to enjoy the performances. So, Lucy proceeds alone for dinner. Coming out of the dinner hall, she stands at the deck of the ship and watched the starry night to de-stress her mind. However she does not know that when she will reach the cabin, an Ides of AI will fall upon her.

THE IDES OF AI

In tired steps, Lucy progresses towards her cabin. Suddenly she discovers that a ray of light is coming from the ajar door of the adjoining cabin, which is occupied by Faith. Startled, she asks herself – 'Why this cabin is open? I thought Faith will be going to the cultural night after dinner!!'

Lucy remembers Faith telling her that she will not come to cabin now and will watch the performances. 'Was Faith not sharing her plans with me, or there is a break-in in her room?' But the later idea being quite improbable, she quickly drops the same from her mind.

Innumerable questions start to muddle up Lucy's mind. Is she feeling unwell? But then her immediate course of action would have been to call Lucy and approach the medical team on the ship. And then Lucy suddenly remembers, Faith has never fallen sick since childhood. Ever.

With growing anxiety, Lucy silently walks towards Faith's cabin. Suddenly, she hears two male voices inside. One of them laughs and says – 'Let us take all these strategic move files from this gadget for tomorrow's final match'. Lucy gets an uncanny feeling. She cautiously peeps through the door. Little did she know, that she will see the Ides of AI.

It seems like a big conspiracy is unfolding in front of her eyes. With horror, Lucy observes that Faith is transferring all the secrete chess move files in her chip to two AI representatives from the satellite team, who usually sit behind Raghav during the games and constantly advise him.

Lucy cannot control the manifestation of her lacrymynal glands which automatically soaks and wets her eyes. A trail of visual memories of the time that she has spent together with Faith keeps playing in her mind. 'I've not known her after all', she thinks bitterly.

Lucy controls herself and moves towards her cabin, unable to decide her next course of action. She gets in her room and waits for the sound of door closing in Faith's cabin. As soon as the sound comes after a while, she moves out of her cabin and watches the two men leaving Faith's room and heading down the corridor. Lucy starts following them through the various passages of the ship. Finally the two men arrive at the cabin of the main player of the satellite, Raghav, with the small copied chip still in their possession. Lucy can imagine that the chip must be containing all the secret files and decides that she has to snatch it at any cost to save humanity from AI intrusion on earth.

Deeply worried and unsure of the course of action, Lucy comes back to her cabin and starts thinking hard. Initially her mind was full of despair, but now that phase is over. 'There must be a way out', she keeps telling herself. Once the thought of approaching Madhyam and other council of earth members comes to her mind, but she discounts the idea immediately. 'I've repeatedly insisted to Madhyam for including Faith in our team. It is my responsibility to solve this.'

In a flash, Lucy suddenly realizes the purpose of including the simulation exercises in the training programme. It has been devised to make her understand the purpose of life, something that can make her **P-R-O-U-D**. If this treachery of Faith leads to the defeat of the earth team and Lucy just lets that happen as a passive by-standing onlooker, she will never be able to forgive herself.

She also remembers the experience of Mr. Morel in the simulation, who did not backtrack from his mission by looking at the name and designation of his adversary. He simply did what he believed to be morally, ethically right. Lucy realizes, Faith might be her friend, but her action tonight has transformed her to an enemy of the mankind. She must be countered for what she has done.

Lucy realized that she is not simply angry with Faith. She is also curious to know why Faith commits such a betrayal. There must be a good reason!!

With greeted teeth, Lucy makes a resolve and decides to confront Faith, but only appealing to her friendliness and willingness to help her. Confrontation will not serve the purpose here. But perhaps tomorrow she must try to learn the reason behind Faith's betrayal.

She goes back to Faith's cabin and knocks on her door. Faith opens the door with a very sleepy appearance and exclaims – 'Lucy! At this hour - '

Before she finishes the sentence, Lucy interjects- 'Yes, I really got late in coming to you. May be I should have come earlier but I thought you are still enjoying the cultural night.'

'Yes, I was there and returned only a few minutes back'. Faith answers with a straight face, to Lucy's growing disbelief.

Lucy asks for Faith' permission to come inside. Stepping aside from the doorframe, Faith asks – 'Sure.. But are you alright?'

Lucy assures her by saying – 'Oh, everything is fine. I just want to chat with you to comfort myself. As tomorrow's deciding game is very important for humanity, I'm feeling a bit nervous and so felt an urge to talk to you.'

'Of course' - reaffirms Faith in a very friendly tone.

Soon they get engaged in a light conversation. However, after sometime Lucy comes to her prime agenda with caution and asks Faith – 'Can you tell me something?'

'Yes, just go ahead' - Faith replies back.

'Are you aware of the fact that there might be secret number codes to each of our rooms by which our rooms can be opened from outside, even when we have locked it from inside?' Lucy asks.

When Faith remains silent with a blank expression on her face, she further goes on, 'This is because we are constantly being observed and monitored by AIs from Elios. My hunch is the council of earth's security team might need to manually override the code to enter a room from outside, in case they suspect something fishy going on inside.'

In reality, Lucy has no proof of this hypothesis but her thought process convinced her this to be a plausible option. So, just as a truth-seeker she makes this wild guess and throws it out to Faith to observe her reaction.

Thinking a while, Faith slowly replies – 'Well I actually overheard about this a few days back, while I was crossing two security guards on the deck. The security guards in the ship are in possession of these codes. But they were telling that this provision is there to help the guests, in case they fall sick.'

Jubilant, Lucy says – 'Bravo, so you need to help me find out the security code number of the cabin of the main player of Satellite, Raghav.'

Faith seems shocked by her expression, 'Oh, what a strange request! But why on earth?'

Lucy coolly answers, 'I've good reasons to ask for this favour'.

'But how I will I do that? It's just not possible. Try to understand this – if the AIs ever get to know this, it will be considered as a diplomatic breach of trust. Negotiations will just be scrapped for ever' - protests Faith.

'Oh really? I would love to see how the council of earth react, when they learn about you transferring the strategic move files in the chip to Raghav', Lucy thinks silently. Aloud she says, 'I don't want to know anything about that. But you have to manage it somehow. Otherwise I will think that you are not my friend, but actually are siding with the satellite. You just want them to win these games', and chuckles innocently.

'Come on Lucy, sometimes you say anything so casually' - Faith complains crossly first but clearly her confidence is shaken. After a few minutes of silent thinking, she says – 'Ok, let me try to get it from one of the security guards who is maintaining the centralized database in the control room of the ship. I 'might be able to do it using my skills of hypnotisation'.

Lucy says – 'Superb - You are the best', and matches her words by hugging and kissing Faith on her forehead.

Faith turns from the door, 'But what do you want to do in Raghav's room in the first place?'

Lucy sports her best innocent smile, 'I've never been to the living quarters of an AI staying in *Elios*. Just want to experience it first-hand.'

It is clear from Faith's expression that she does not believe Lucy's excuse. But she shrugs her shoulders and sets out for the centralized database room. Lucy goes back to her room and waits.

Lucy wonders, 'Will Faith help me, given that she passed the information to Raghav's support team in her own accord?' But then she remembers that Faith has also learned the importance of being '**P-R-O-U-D**' during simulations and the importance of making 'choices' at crucial junctures.

After almost an hour Faith comes back to Lucy's room and tells her the security code. After that, with a wide smile, almost artificial, she asks – 'Can I go to sleep now my little stubborn girl, as it is already 1 a.m. and tomorrow is the day of decider for humanity?'

Lucy embraces Faith and says – 'Thank You'.

Faith goes off to sleep but Lucy does not. She heads towards Raghav's cabin with an overlapping sensation of risk, fear and excitement. Luckily, Raghav is not in the room and the chip is kept on his table, quite casually! So, Lucy does not face any problem in retrieving it. Then she tiptoes back to her room, without anybody noticing her.

Lucy then sits for a long time beside the window, going over all the sweet memories that she shares with Faith in her mind. Her nerves are too tensed to sleep. The night outside starts fading away and the white round moon in the sky begins to make space for the sun in the sky.

THE OUTCOME

The next day begins at 8 a.m. in the negotiation hall, with a thrill of uncertainty looming large. The third and final game that had set in with a slow defensive pace is poised with an equal chance for both earth and satellite to win. The final day is a crucial day, with profound implications for the sustainability negotiations and future of humanity.

The satellite side starts attacking from the beginning in a manner as if they are well aware of the possible moves of the earth team. The earth team is not able to understand how the satellite team can be so much aware of their strategic moves. Only Lucy can sense it - Raghav must have immediately copied the contents of Faith's chip yesterday and that's why he is so calm even after losing the same. So, whenever Faith is suggesting a move, out of the ones stored in the chip, the satellite team is working out all the possible strategies on that basis. After almost three hours of defence, the earth team starts getting slowly but conclusively cornered. At this juncture, the lunch bell comes as a rescue. In the lunchtime, Madhyam comes to Lucy and Faith and seeks their help.

Madhyam implores, with a strong undercurrent of urgency in his voice, - 'Lucy and Faith, you have to work out some moves post lunch to win it for us. Otherwise, we are doomed in the negotiation.'

Lucy silently thinks, 'My Morel moment has come! I cannot delay it further.' Taking a deep breath, Lucy tells Madhyam in a decided tone – 'Yes, we need to do something about the game. But, it will be done by myself and NOT Faith. There is no need for her to advise N'Cono during the post-lunch session. She can just be a spectator.'

Faith gets angry and stares at Lucy with disbelieving eyes – 'How can you be so arrogant and megalomaniac?'

Lucy knows that she has to confront Faith now. She retorts in a measured yet sad tone – 'Because Faith, I know you can't save humanity and you were never meant to save us.'

Before Faith can say anything, Madhyam, who wore a puzzled look so far during the confrontation, comes to a decision and says – 'Ok Lucy, I agree. Just sit with N'Cono and work the strategies out as we have to save humanity post lunch. And Faith, you've heard Lucy. She must be having a good reason for placing such an odd request. I'm also curious to know the reasons from her later. But right now, just comply with it.'

Lucy skips lunch and sits with her electronic gadget studying some of the strategic chess moves in her cabin for ten minutes. She then takes a deep breath and takes a crucial call. From now on, she is not going to follow the codes included in the chip. That's what the satellite team is going to expect as an obvious course of action for the earth team. Then she approaches the room of N'Cono. While everybody takes lunch, two of them sit in the room, takes just some light juice to maintain the body fluid and prepares for the post lunch game.

Lucy tries to arrange her thought process in a game theoretic manner. If the AIs from satellite do not know about the fact that she knows about the transfer of files, they will feel comfortable and proceed with their natural game. Actually, they will prefer to play a more attacking game, as they are doing now. And, in case they come to know about Lucy's knowledge about the theft, will they be concerned? In all probability not. They have contempt for the thought process and action of the humans and will expect Lucy to immediately share the news with everybody. As a result, the earth team will be nervous, and are bound to commit mistakes, once cornered.

Lucy realizes under no circumstances the AIs will expect the earth team to be unduly offensive. So, she decides that post-lunch the earth team must start with an attacking mode, once they come out from the current situation. N'Cono is naturally surprised to hear Lucy's views, but Lucy persists. Finally, N'Cono agrees to follow her suggestions, though with a sense of unease.

In the first hour of the post lunch session, the earth team carefully defends their castle quite well and slowly comes out of the cornered situation, moving towards a draw. However, the surprise element comes just one hour before the close of the day.

Suddenly, the earth team starts attacking in a way as if correctly anticipating the next 30 moves of the satellite team. Lucy try to push her abilities beyond the frontier under the pressure scenario, and seeing her example everybody in the earth team, including Eman and Ivan, appropriately rise to the occasion. The Satellite team out of the shock could not adjust to their moves and starts making mistakes. They are faced with their first check just thirty minutes before the close of the play. In an utter state of disbelief, the satellite team starts looking towards each other. A similar disbelief also gets spread onto the spectators in the hall who cannot even believe the turnaround. Obviously, among the spectators, supporters of earth enjoy this turnaround while the AIs from the satellite feel dejected and sit silently.

A little relaxed, Lucy now turns towards Faith who was sitting silently among the earth team members since lunch, and conveys – 'Time is the only resource in the space, galaxy and universe and it can turn around anytime'.

Faith realizes the subtext, gets up and says – 'I have to go to the rest room'.

'Or to the satellite, as you always were theirs' - Retorts Lucy in a low voice so that the surrounding members of the earth team in the excitement of the moment fail to hear.

Faith becomes restless with a rarest glimpse of the feeling that Lucy has hardly ever seen in her and it is called- 'Agitation'. Judging from her expressions, Lucy fears she will hit back sharply. But she prefers to remain silent.

After sitting beside Lucy for a few seconds with a lost expression on her face, Faith starts moving towards the restroom in one corner of the negotiation hall.

By this time, earth has consecutively given five checks to AI team and the sixth one finally leads to check mate, denying the dreams of the council of satellite to form a green settlement on earth.

Sounds of jubilation, clamour and clapping from representatives of all the income groups and people of earth fills up the air.

Lucy sees Lazarus standing at a distance, his head slightly stooping: a very expression unexpected from his personality and speech on the first day in the ship. He is surrounded by a few satellite representatives, who are speaking in low voices. Is he dejected? Barbara is also standing among the group, apparently deep in thought, lost, a little dejected but not broken. Her jawline says, 'The game is lost, but the negotiation is not'.

She also sees Jack, Madhyam and Bruke embracing each other passionately and shouting energetically. 'Too beautiful a sight for the eyes', Lucy thought, 'for the sake of mankind, I hope this harmony among the income groups will now persist'.

But where is Faith?

Lucy rushes towards the rest room to find out Faith. She cannot find Faith in the rest room. Then she runs towards *Faith's* cabin which is surprisingly open. Inside, she discovers a note written by Faith for her on the table adjoining to the bed.

The note, written in a hurry, but carrying a detailed thought, proceeds in the following manner-

'Dear Lucy - my affection, love and the cause of contradiction,

By the time, you find this note, I will be transported to a future time zone of the council of AI who have been watching everybody on satellite and earth. The exploration from the future time zone to earth began quite some time back, almost 20 years before. Many of us like me were programmed in the future time zone of the council of AI in a distant planet and were sent to earth and satellite. I was programmed and sent to earth for this negotiation day. I knew the day the negotiation will be over, I will be called back and transported immediately in a flash of second by means of a time transportation gadget. Our objective was not to influence the regular day-to-day events that may unduly alter history, but create a more amenable path from the satellite's perspective altogether. As our creators told me, 'you are being sent to save the planet earth from self-destruction'.

So, I arrived on earth, was raised in a family of AI here through a biological maturing process, and met you, after my so-called parents were recalled back to the future time zone. I became a lone refugee on earth with a mission of helping Raghav in the chess game. Then I met you, I loved you dearly like a friend, but given my collective memory from the future and your young and passionate energy, I always emotionally felt like a mother to you. But I was programmed to help the AIs against humanity! So, my love and mission both were equally true to my logical mind and yet the contradiction surfaced. Despite my friendship to you, I stayed on course of my primary mission: 'Help Raghav'. However, yesterday night, in the ship when you asked me of the security code, I immediately became aware of the reason behind it. But as per my mission, I am not supposed to show that I was aware of your thought process. If it comes to your knowledge that I know that you know my action, it might pre-shadow your next moves. We are not supposed to let that happen. It may seriously alter the course of history and jeopardise our plans.

I secretly followed you to Raghav's cabin, saw that you stole the chip from there but did not say or do anything even though instructions had come to me through our time connecting gadgets to kill or cerebrally disable you last night. It would have been a continuation of their style of function, as long back a human called Dr. Dang was killed by them through their agents on earth as he was becoming a threat to their desire of controlling an empire of AI, based on sustainable practices, in this galaxy. Dr. Dang's experiments, which could have made human minds superior, was proceeding to hinder their plan which the council of AI from future time zone did not want. After all the humans are susceptible to unsustainable practices.

History repeats itself, and likewise, the instructions came from future time zone of AI council heads to eliminate you. This time they feared if human settlement comes in the satellite, the galactic pollution may increase in long run, because, as a race, humans are susceptible to temptations. But I could not listen to them, as besides being an AI spy I was emotionally like your mother and friend as well. Moreover, a lifetime among you all, the human folk, has enabled me to realize that humans evolve, but AIs upgrade. So, in response to the received instructions my logical conscience cried, 'I shall not commit the grievous sin of losing faith', in the inherent and internal good in the mankind.

But as per my pre-decided programme, I had to help Raghav even though I did not follow their instructions to the letter. So when we started losing the game, I prepared to leave as I was constantly receiving signals from them from future to come to my ship cabin for time transportation. Hence, my fate was inevitable. But before the time transportation, I wanted you to know all these contradictions of mine.

You must be wondering by now, 'Why this letter? Does it not bring forward the risk of altering the course of history?' You are very right. Now, I do not want to be bound by my original brief, and want to 'choose' once again. I have been thinking ever since we attended the simulations in the lab. For the first time since my creation, today I can feel the conflict that humans face while taking their decisions. Their dilemma is touching - they surely deserve another chance!!

By this time, I am on way to future, and an alternate history path perhaps will now be created. With more informed knowledge and improved insight, you might be instrumental in writing new chapter codes for a Protocol between humans and AIs. Possibly someday we will meet again in future.

Leave the letter on the table, Lucy. Once your touch is removed from the surface of the paper, this will auto-destruct in 30 seconds.'

The note abruptly comes to an end. Lucy lets out a sigh and her heart suddenly feels a sense of vacuum. Until reading this letter, Lucy felt that she understands the AI mind like the palm of her hand, but now she becomes aware of her limitations. It nevertheless flashes in her mind, 'This moment, no other human comprehends the possible evolution of the AI mind, like me.'

She also now better comprehends the true lessons of the simulation exercises, and appreciates what makes one **P-R-O-U-D**. She closes her eyes and thinks of General Choltitz, who disobeyed his order because he correctly understood the importance of protecting something valuable, with an ever-lasting impression on human civilization. Faith has just opened a new avenue for the mankind through her decision. It will surely be making the AIs of the future infuriated but that did not stop Faith from undertaking a course of action that appealed to her sense of pride. But to what extent her intervention will alter the course of the history? Will mankind learn from their past mistakes?

Lucy laughs, even in the midst of the mounting tensions, from her astounding discovery. Faith wrote in her letter, 'Humans evolve, but AIs upgrade'!! How can one explain *Faith's* belief in humans then? Touch of human heart wining over and transforming cold lifeless AI logic?

With a hissing sound the letter, kept on the table, vanishes in thin air. This bring Lucy out of her reverie. She wonders, 'What to do now?'

After a few minutes thinking, Lucy realizes she cannot share this development with anybody, not even Madhyam. Without the letter of Faith, in all probability, everybody will consider her story a practical joke and make fun of her. In the celebration mode, nobody will bother to attribute much on *Faith's* sudden disappearance. Faith, an expert on human psychology, knew this perfectly and that's why dared to be candid with her.

On the other extreme, if her account is believed, then it will create an enormous animosity between the humans and AIs. Worse, it'll immediately create mistrust among the humans and a riot will follow. People will start accusing each other that they are AI spies! That will indeed have course correction, but a very undesirable one and the alternate history Faith imagined, would never materialize.

Lucy now fully comprehends the difference between the actions of Alexander the Great and General Pollock after a victory in a war. The AIs are and will continue to be a threat to the humankind. Today's negotiation was just the beginning of a long battle. But their commitment to environment is genuine. 'Should we make them feel further antagonized through our actions?', Lucy silently asks herself and the answer becomes obvious.

'Why don't we urge the AIs for not just allowing the humans re-entry in the satellite, but also go beyond? Why not push them for technology transfer for transforming the earth settlements, especially in *Domus* and *the Reef*, who otherwise have limited resources to further sustainable development goals? Why not force them at the negotiation table to remove the restrictive condition on humans on inter-planetary travel? Rather they should help us with technology so that our future satellites on the moon to begin with and across the galaxy in long run become environmentally sustainable, unlike our first adventure', waves of thought keeps coming to Lucy's mind and she cannot wait to share them with the council of earth.

She suddenly remembers the experience of North Korea in the simulation and realizes that in the case of disagreement over ideology and policy implementation, the solution is never found in isolation but only through proactive engagement.

She comes out of *Faith's* cabin and walks back towards the negotiation hall. As she approaches towards the hall, the joy, celebration of the residents of this planet earth becomes more prominent in the background as humanity is waiting for a new Protocol for earth and satellite, the have and have nots in the technology plane. Slowly and steadily, Lucy makes her steps for the hall waiting for the future to unfold. On the way, she looks up towards the sky. It feels as if, the canopy full of stars, sends a silent invitation to her. Suddenly the starry night starts fading in front of her eyes, and a wrapper of darkness engulfs Lucy. From a distance, she hears someone asking repeatedly, 'Lucy are you all right?'

BACK HOME

October 7, 2016
00.12 hrs

'Lucy are you all right?' the words echo in the mind of Lucy once again.

She finally opens her eyes and stare directly to the anxious-looking face of Mrs. Jenny Dang.

'Thank god, you are opening your eyes now. In the house of Jacobs, we went to the movie-room after an hour or so and found you sound asleep. I was a little concerned but Peter and Maria explained that you must have been very tired after a busy day at the school. They helped me to put you in the car. In fact Peter drove us home and put you on the bed. You were sound asleep throughout. Its 11.50 p.m. in the night now. I was really worried whether to call a doctor.' Mrs. Dang lets out her anxieties without taking a pause.

Lucy nods and gets up on the bed. She is feeling little light in the head, but otherwise feels quite refreshed.

'You must have a glass of milk first', decides Mrs. Dang and leaves the room.

Lucy closes her eyes and thinks hard. She is trying to grasp the meaning of her strange visions. Was it a dream or it wasn't? Was she really witnessing the events of the future and participating in the events? And what is the significance of the fact that she is retaining her memories? Are her actions going to alter the course of history in coming days?

'God, I am only a ten-year old girl! How am I going to handle this'? She mutters.

She dearly misses her father, Dr. Jonathan Dang, every day and night for the last couple of months. And she does not feel like going to the park again. Today, the knowledge obtained during her surreal journey during the trance is even more astounding!

To brush off the uneasy thoughts, Lucy gets up and moves to the drawing room. Wandering aimlessly, she picks up the paper and reads the headline, 'Countries across the income group are going to honour the Paris Climate Change Deal'.

'I wish', Lucy mutters under her breath, 'the future as I witnessed never comes. But the letter of Faith, and the possibility of... No I don't even want to think about that'.

THE LAB

October 7, 2016
00.15 hrs

Suddenly, lights are put on and the screens go black in the simulation lab. Dr. Jacob realizes that he is sitting in the same chair for the last three hours. The stream of events were too intense for him even to occasionally stretch his muscles. He now gets up and sports a weary smile, glancing towards his colleagues. They were also working in the lab tirelessly for the last couple of hours.

While wiping the glasses of his spec with the lab apron, Dr. Jacob cleans his throat and announces, 'I think Lucy is now ready for her next level of experience.

Dr. Maria Jacob quietly says, 'What about the other special children?'

Dr. Peter Jacob nods and tells the scientists standing around him, 'The possibilities of alternate course of future are now becoming wider. So, maybe next time we'll check the feasibility and practicality of fathoming the psychological journey of another child along with Lucy'.

One scientist hurriedly notes down a few points in his diary.

Dr. Maria Jacob asks, 'What is our takeaway this time, Peter?'

Dr. Peter Jacob sighs and shakes his head in an uncertain manner, 'What we heard during the experiment is fascinating. So far we thought that we are taking a look into the future and learning from our future past mistakes, will be able to avert the damage.'

'The age-old adage saying "ignorance is bliss" is proved once again. We now know that the AIs of the plausible future can look back in our times and can even send their agents to intervene and influence current events. Our poor track record of environmental management is nothing but an irritation for them.'

'So, we must go for the next level of experiment. We have to know what would happen in the plausible future in the subsequent period, after the negotiation of the protocol. Would the AIs help the mankind to implement sustainable practices on earth? Would they continue to deny us the flexibility to migrate to distant planets? More importantly, would environmental cost be internalized in all our future decisions?'

A scientist named Dr. Ghosh comments, 'At least now we have a plausible explanation of Dr. Dang's murder. It's unsettling.'

Several scientists silently nod in agreement. Dr. Maria Jacob drily remarks, 'Well, now we can understand why the cops were never able to identify the murderer.'

Dr. Peter Jacob lets out a hollow laugh and repeats, 'Ignorance is bliss'.

After a few moments, he looks at everyone and says, 'Well, let me just go back to my office. I've to write down the possible steps that need to be taken urgently to control global emissions. Tomorrow we must share them, along with today's experiment results, with our Board of Directors. We cannot afford to delay it.'

Another scientist named Dr. Richards asks in an uncertain voice, 'But surely, the plausible future that we've witnessed just now may not be repeated exactly?'

Dr. Maria Jacob answers, 'True, but given the unsolved murder of Dr. Dang and the plausible explanations we came across today, nothing can be left to chances.'

Almost all the scientists mutter in agreement.

Dr. Ghosh comments, 'Our Board of Directors will not be happy to hear the results of this experiment'.

Dr. Peter Jacob just sighs.

Dr. Chang, who was silent so far, asks, 'So, when shall we start for the next experiment?'

With a rare show of emotion, Dr. Jacob answers, 'As early as possible. From tomorrow morning. Did you not hear yesterday's news on global GHG emissions? The irreversible damages are killing the planet.'

Dr. Chang protests, 'But we have to synchronize the experiences of another child along with Lucy in the next experiment, it'll take some time. We just cannot rush into it'.

Dr. Peter Jacob gets up and moves towards the lab door. Everybody notice that he suddenly looks older. They remember he is now going back to his office to write the report.

Turning from the lab door, he says in a tired voice, 'Al right, proceed with the necessary caution to secure precision. But remember another age-old adage, "time and tide wait for none". And, time is fast running out for the humankind.'

NOTE ON THE TIMELINE OF LUCY'S JOURNEY

Date / Time	Month	Year	Event
		2015	Lucy goes to the Park and after drinking the potion and be a part of Simulation one
		2015	Dr. Jonathan Dang dies the very night, when Lucy was exposed to Simulation one
7	October	2016	Lucy goes to the Dr. Jacob's house and be a part of Simulation two
		2100	Ice Age sets in
1	January	2150	Lucy boards the Train in Simulation one, when ice age was prevailing in the world
	May	2150	The temperature in the world start rising
		2155	Reclaimed islands formed by the elites

		2160	Middle-income and Climate refugees emerge as the two groups residing in the single landmass
		2170	Super-elites emerge as an income group in the reclaimed islands, who start aspiring for a home in the sky
		2180	New satellite built and launched in the orbit
		2190	Satellite starts violating environmental stainability, with compromise in environmental impact assessment
		2200	AIs of another galaxy under the leadership of Lazarus arrive at the satellite, who were tracking the developments on earth for the last three millennium
		2200-05	Formation of Council of Satellite consisting of representatives from both humans and AIs, who start investigations on environmental irregularities

	March	2205	Deportation of all the super-elites, who either flouted the environmental norms or had some business links with the elites compromising on these fronts, to earth
	March	2205	Only the super-elites with proven track records of adopting sustainable practices and intellectual prowess like the scientists were allowed to remain on the satellite
		2230	The underground island lab built on earth to comprehend the limits of AI mind
31	January	2249	All the remaining super-elites were forced to return from the satellite to the smart island cities due to their declining importance and prospects
		2249	AIs objected to the idea of elites creating another satellite in space
		2249	AIs objected to the idea of elites creating a colony in moon

	April - July	2249	Emergence of unity across all income groups against the AI oppression, denying mankind a foothold in the satellite
	August	2249	Formation of Council of Earth, with Jack, Madhyam and Bruke representing elites, middle-income and climate refugee groups respectively
	September - December	2249	Growing voice across all income groups in earth against AI policy and demand for a new Protocol
	November-December	2049	Attempts begin to create more artificial smart islands to accommodate the population pressure among the elites
31	January	2250	Lucy speaks with Madhyam in second simulation
2	February	2250	The AIs discuss the modalities of the negotiation and officially launches the same
First week	March	2250	Preparations for negotiations
Last Week	March	2250	Week 1 of the Training for the earth participants in the negotiation, including Lucy

First Week	April	2250	Week 2 of the Training follows for Lucy
Second Week	April	2250	Lucy and other earth participants receive training on chess moves
Third Week	May	2250	Lucy and Faith go to the island to visit the cave and underground laboratory
	May	2250	The negotiation venue, a ship called 'Noah' is prepared for the event
First week	June	2250	The negotiation takes place, resulting in victory for mankind

NOTE TO THE CHARACTERS IN THE NARRATIVE

Character	Type	Origin / Residence	Note
Barbara	AI	Another Galaxy	Came from a planet in another galaxy to the satellite. Presently Deputy Council Chair of Satellite.
Bruke	Human	Climate refugee territory	Head of the Council of the climate refugee colony.
Chang	Human	Present day New York	A scientist at the Simulation lab.
Donald	Human	Smart islands	An elite and presently Head of the Protocol Secretariat.
Eman	Human	Smart islands	An elite specializing in strategic thinking and cognitive part of human brain, who was selected as a member of the earth's negotiating team.

Faith	AI	Sent by AI council of the future	Friend of Lucy, who stayed in her neighbourhood to gain her confidence. She specialized in understanding the application of conscious, subconscious and unconscious conscience in AIs.
Ghosh	Human	Present day New York	A scientist at the Simulation lab.
Iris	AI	Another Galaxy	Presently residing at the satellite. Deputy of Donald at the Protocol Secretariat.
Ivan	Human	Climate refugee territory	Studied at the smart islands on a scholarship. Specializes in non-cognitive learning abilities of human brain. Selected as a member of the earth's negotiating team.
Jack	Human	Smart islands	Head of the Council of the elites residing at the smart islands.
Jenny Dang	Human	Present day New York	Mother of Lucy. An author and activist on sustainability issues.

Jonathan Dang	Human	Present day New York	Father of Lucy. A scientist, who conducted an experiment through Lucy's mind to understand the future sustainability challenges.
Kate	Human	Middle Income Group	Chief simulation scientist at the special training centre constructed by the council of earth.
Lazarus	AI	Another Galaxy	Came from a planet in another galaxy to the satellite. Presently Council Chair of Satellite.
Liam and Emiko	AI	Island laboratory	Humanoid AIs of the latest design, constructed at the island lab. Used by the humans to understand various aspects of AI thought process.
Lucy	Human	Present day New York	A ten-year old girl living in New York. The protagonist of the story. Through her visions in the experiment, the team of scientists are trying to understand the future sustainability challenges.
Madhyam	Human	Middle Income Group	Head of the Council of the Middle Income Group.

Maria Jacob	Human	Present day New York	The wife of Dr. Jacob and a scientist. Actively participates in the experiments. Devoted to the cause of environmental sustainability.
N'Cono	Human	Smart islands	A super-elite, who was selected as the chess player to represent earth.
Paul	Human	Middle Income Group	Simulation scientist working at the special training centre constructed by the council of earth.
Pedro	Human	Island laboratory	Chief scientist at the island Lab.
Peter Jacob	Human	Present day New York	The deputy of Dr. Jonathan Dang. After death of Dr. Dang, takes the initiative and experiments forward. Devoted to the cause of environmental sustainability.
Raghav	AI	Another Galaxy	Chess player selected to represent the satellite.
Richards	Human	Present day New York	A scientist at the Simulation lab.
Rishi	Human	Middle Income Group	Lead Trainer at the University training centre.

Valentina, Akil and Indra	AI	Island laboratory	Humanoid AIs of the first successful prototype batch, constructed at the island lab. Used by the humans to understand various aspects of AI thought process.

NOTE ON THE HISTORICAL / MYTHOLOGICAL CHARACTERS

Character	Note
Achilles	The mythological half-god, the hero of the Trojan war in the Greek classic Iliad. He killed the Trajon prince Hector at the battle. Alexander the Great used to worship Achilles since childhood after reading his achievements and exploits in the battle.
Alexander the Great	Alexander the Great became the King of Macedon at young age after the death of his father King Philip II. He was taught by Aristotle in his childhood. He led the conquest of the Greek army that defeated the Persian King Darius III. After conquering the Persian empire, his army won the Battle of the Hydaspes in India. Though initially intent to move further east, he decided to return home. En route, he died in Babylon in 323 BC. At the time of death, his empire was spread over an enormous landmass in Africa, Asia and Europe.

Darius III	Darius III, the last king of the Achaemenid empire of Persia, was defeated by Alexander the Great. It is said that he abandoned his forces at the Battle of Gaugamela (331 BC).
General Dietrich von Choltitz	Geenral Choltitz was a German army officer during World War II. As the commander of Nazi-occupied Paris in 1944, he received a direct order from Hitler to destroy the level the city before retreat. However, he defied the same and surrendered the city to Free French forces.
Mr. Edmund Dene Morel	Mr. Morel was a British journalist, later turned author and politician, who brought to public notice the existence of slavery in King Leopold's Congo and actively campaigned against it. His renowned contributions include *King Leopold's Rule in Africa, The Black Man's Burden* etc.
General George Pollock	General Pollock was a renowned British Indian army officer, who was given the command of the British force to rescue British hostages after the First Anglo-Afghan war of 1842. His campaigns were successful in Jalalabad and Kabul. Before the retreat from Kabul, his troops destroyed the famous Char Chatta Bazaar in 1842.

Hector	The Trajon prince and their bravest worrier who gets killed by Achilles in the Greek classic *Iliad*. As per the mythology, after killing him in the duel Achilles tied Hector's dead body with his chariot and drove the same.
Kim Il-sung	President Kim Il-sung emerged as the Supreme Leader of North Korea, where he ruled over 1948 to 1994. A personality cult evolved during his period. After the fall of USSR in the post-cold war period, the country faced greater hardships. The rule of President Kim has been followed by the reign of his son Kim Jong-il and grandson Kim Jong-un.
King Leopold II	The longest serving Belgian Monarch, King Leopold II managed to receive control of Congo Free State, his exclusive private project, through international recognition during Berlin Conference, 1885. But the excessive focus on ivory and rubber led to forced labour and slavery, which over the period was noticed by the world. The writings of Mr. Morel and others turned the opinion and finally in 1908, the King transferred the control of the colony to Belgium.

Nicola Tesla	Nikola Tesla was born in a Serbian family in modern Croatia and came to US in 1884. He was an inventor, with profound knowlwdge in electrical and mechanical engineering. He initially joined Edison Machine Works and went on to form Tesla Electric Light &Manufacturing. Tesla, who always dreamt of clean energy and future, was ahead of his time. He died in 1943.
Porus	Porus, an Indian King from the Indus valley bravely fought against Alexander the Great but was defeated in the Battle of the Hydaspes (326 BC). Even on the face of certain defeat, he did not abandon his troops, which earned Alexander's appreciation. Hugely impressed with his bravery and leadership quality, the Greek King allowed Porus to reign over his kingdom and the adjoining lands as a satrap.

www.ingramcontent.com/pod-product-compliance
Lightning Source LLC
Chambersburg PA
CBHW061239170626
46809CB00007B/2745